M000206036

by
Chance

REBECCA
BRICKER

Folio&Leaf

By Chance

ISBN-10: 0998277010
ISBN-13: 978-0998277011

Folio & Leaf Publishing
USA

Cover design by JD Smith Design

How many times in our lives do we turn away from love – or the possibility of it?

Sometimes the prospect of love comes in a fleeting moment that we might miss altogether. Or it gets lost in the conversation we *don't* have with someone who catches our eye.

Love can barge into the room at the wrong time. Or it can tiptoe in and take us pleasantly by surprise.

If we bar the door, it might not come knocking at all.

I dedicate this book to those longing for love,
with the hope that, just by chance,
the wonder and mystery of it
will find you – and delight you –
when you least expect it.

ALSO BY REBECCA BRICKER

Tales from Tavanti:
An American Woman's Mid-Life Adventure in Italy

Not a True Story

The Secret of Marie

The Sound of His Voice

I sometimes think about that Sunday afternoon in Florence and wonder WHAT IF.

The piazza in my neighborhood was buzzing with chatter and laughter and the first heady hints of spring that day.

As I walked away from the flower stand, carrying a bouquet of daffodils, I saw him watching me.

He was short, slight, middle-aged, with pudgy, rosy cheeks and spectacles. And he wore a fedora.

I looked at this bespectacled voyeur in his fedora and pretended he was Marcello Mastroianni, pulling on a cigarette with fire in his eyes. My life in Italy had done nothing to quiet my romantic inclinations.

I would have kept walking except that this man demanded my full attention. "*Signora...*" he said tenderly as he approached me.

He raised a hand as if to cup my face, then rested it on his chest, presumably to quiet his thumping heart.

I could have given him a dirty look or worse. I have a male friend in Florence who does a funny imitation of me scowling at him on the night we met, when he followed me out of a bookstore wanting to talk to me.

So much hangs in the balance with chance encounters. You have to decide in an instant if you've come face to face with a pervert or a nice guy you'd like to have in your life.

I looked intently at this man, trying to find a clue in his eyes. He wanted me to have coffee with him. If not today, another time. I hesitated when he asked how he could reach me. Would I give him my phone number? "*Non è possibile?*" he said. It was more of a plea than a question.

In the piazza on that spring afternoon, love was all around. Couples kissed. Friends embraced. Children ran gleefully into their parents' arms. I felt a tug on my heartstrings.

But I shook my head and said to him, "I'm sorry. It is not possible." From our very brief conversation, I already had sensed complications. He didn't live in the city and didn't have internet access. Hardly a fair measure of this man, I know.

He nodded sadly and then kissed me on each cheek. For an instant, he could have been Marcello and we could have been lovers in an Italian movie.

I'll never know what might have come of that encounter if I had said YES.

But I walked away smiling. It was a lovely spring day in Florence and *amore* was everywhere. In that moment, that was enough for me.

~ 1 ~

The gloves

Life in Italy wasn't always romantic. I often cursed its inefficiency and bureaucracy and the general indifference to it all. Actually, the indifference was a coping mechanism, but I struggled to master the technique. I come from a culture of convenience and customer service – foreign concepts in a country that charms foreigners with its well-branded image of *la dolce vita*.

One hot summer afternoon, my frustration boiled over at the taxi stand near my apartment. Surprisingly, there were taxis there that day – but none of them had drivers. They all were on a coffee break at the bar across the street.

Another woman waited with me, both of us on our phones trying to get a dispatcher to answer at one of Florence's two taxi companies. We had their numbers on speed dial: 055 4242 and 055 4390. Hailing a cab on the street in Florence is a crapshoot. If you want a taxi, you go to a taxi stand (also a crapshoot) or call (often an exercise in futility).

It was a moment of shared exasperation as we both got busy signals. "Nothing in this country works," she lamented.

I was surprised to hear her American accent. She had perfected the look of a chic *italiana* in her crisp linen and designer accessories.

"How long have you lived here?" I asked.

"Eight years." She shook her head. "But I'm done."

Just then, a taxi dispatcher answered my call. I held my breath when she put me on hold. The ultimate cruelty is a recorded message saying there are no taxis available. One day, I spent a half hour calling for a cab to take me to the airport. When a dispatcher finally answered, I could hear the indifference in his voice as he told me there were no taxis.

"When will there be taxis?" My flight was leaving in less than two hours.

"Today is busy. Maybe tomorrow."

I clicked off and shouted at my phone, "BUT I WANT TO FLY TO PARIS TODAY!"

I had emotionally linked arms with my compatriot at the taxi stand and when my cab arrived, I waited until the driver called the dispatcher and confirmed another taxi was on its way to pick her up. When I finally leaned back against the seat, perspiration blotting my shirt, I felt only marginally victorious.

I eventually learned a secret about Florence's taxi culture. If you're ever stuck on the street and can't get through to a dispatcher, find a hotel and ask the front desk or concierge to call a cab for you. They often have online access and get immediate results.

The same was true at the sports clinic where I had been going for chiropractic treatments for an ankle I had twisted on Florence's wobbly ancient cobbles. I rarely had to wait more than three minutes for a cab after my appointments.

One February evening, my taxi pulled up across the street from the clinic. The driver motioned to me, wanting to know which direction we needed to go. I pointed in the direction he had come from, so he pulled into the clinic's driveway. It was a big taxi with sliding doors. I said *buonasera* and gave him my address as I got in the cab and struggled to close the door. He reached over the back of the front seat to help me, but after a second try, I succeeded.

"There!" I said.

"Are you English?"

"No. American."

As he backed up and turned the cab around, he asked, "Would you prefer to speak in Italian or English?"

I smiled. "My English is really good. My Italian, not so much."

His English was great. He wanted to know what brought me to Florence.

"I'm a writer."

"What do you write?"

"Novels mostly. I just finished a book about an art forgery and part of the story takes place in Florence."

"So that's why you're here. How do you like Florence?"

"It's a beautiful city." I didn't voice my opinion about the taxi system.

"Where are you from in America?"

"California."

"Ah, California." He said that with the wistfulness I often hear when I tell Italians where I'm from. "Life is very different here."

"Yes, it is. But I like many of the differences." That was true.

"Tell me what you like."

"I like the rhythm of the day. It's less hurried and stressful here. Have you lived in Florence long?" I asked.

"My whole life. Can you imagine? I will be 55 this year. I have never lived anywhere else."

"Is all your family here?"

"Yes. We live outside Florence now. It's easier when you have children in school."

"How old are your children?"

"My son is 31 and has a baby now. My daughter is 17." He quickly added, "I'm divorced."

I could see only the side of this man's face – just his right ear and a bit of his right cheek. I hadn't gotten a good look at him when I got in the cab because I had been twisted sideways trying to get the door to slide shut.

"What about your family?" he asked.

"I've lost my parents and sister," I said quietly. "I have a son and I miss him terribly."

I could hear the air go out of his lungs, as if he felt my pain. "How old is your son?"

"Twenty-seven."

"Where does he live?"

"San Francisco."

"How often do you see him?"

"Not often enough."

"How long will you stay in Florence?" the driver asked.

"I need to decide that soon. My visa is coming up for renewal."

"Do you want to stay?"

"It's not an easy decision. I've made many friends here. Florence feels like a second home to me now."

"You are young. Your life is full of possibilities, *si?*"

"I'm older than you are."

"That isn't possible."

"I am."

"You look like you're in your forties."

"I'm not."

"Seriously?"

I laughed. "When a woman tells you she's older than you think, you should believe her."

He laughed, too. "People must tell you all the time that you look so young."

"That's nice of you to say."

People often guess I am younger than my years. I attribute that to good genes – my mom didn't have a wrinkle on her face when she died in her mid-80s. But I also have a zest for life that I think keeps the years from taking a toll.

The driver turned onto Ponte Santa Trinita, one of Florence's seven bridges that span the Arno. It was early evening. The sun had already set, leaving a cobalt-blue sky as a backdrop to the famous Ponte Vecchio. The windows of the old bridge's little shops cast flickering golden reflections on the surface of the water below.

I never tired of this view. I thought of all the people who cross Florence's bridges in a day – the streams of tourists and those who live in this beautiful city, some of whom have lived here their entire lives, whose families have lived here for generations.

As he drove down Via dei Serragli, through the heart of Florence's artisan district known as the Oltrarno, he told me a little bit about its history.

I liked this man. When he pulled up at my apartment, I was happy with his last question for me.

"Would you like to meet again?" he asked.

He switched on the overhead light and turned around as I was getting money from my wallet. Before I looked up at him, I knew he was taking me in.

He was handsome, with a stubble-beard and a warm smile. I could see kindness in his eyes and imagined they sparked with mischief from time to time.

"I'd like to see you again, too," I said.

He produced his card. "This is my number and my e-mail. My name is Niccolò."

"It's nice to meet you, Niccolò. I'm Laura."

I gave him a €20 note for the fare and gathered my things. I already had the door open when he handed me the change. He quickly grabbed the handle of his door as if he were going to get out. But he hesitated for a second and looked back at me.

I smiled at him. "I'll text you. Maybe we could have coffee one day when you're in the neighborhood."

"I'd like that," he said.

I didn't sleep well that night. I was getting over a cold and had a cough that kept waking me up. In my sleepless state, I thought about Niccolò.

During my time in Florence, I had dated a few Italian guys. They were incorrigible flirts and great lovers, but they all seemed to have an attachment disorder.

The Italian male psyche mystified me. The men I knew were passionate and craved sex. But Italian men seem to have a warped appreciation for women. They adore their mothers, love their wives, and lust after women who satisfy their sexual appetites. Mistresses and prostitutes are part of Italian life. Italian prostitutes even have unions and pensions.

Infidelity was rampant in Italy, from what I could see, and not only with men. I had several female friends who were cheating on their husbands, who were most likely unfaithful, too. Some of these women weren't happy with their sex lives with their husbands – or the lack of sex – so they discreetly wandered. A lunchtime hotel tryst. A weekend trip with a "girlfriend." A secret e-mail correspondence with an admirer who knew how to make a woman's pulse quicken.

The more I got to know Italian men, the more I appreciated American men. To me, what seemed to be missing in the makeup of the Italian male was good old-fashioned *manners*. Not that Italian men aren't inclined to jump out of a cab and open the door for you. But there's a malignant disregard for the courtesy of a reply to a simple text message or a call the next day after sharing your bed the night before. By withholding their attention and affection, they seem to think you'll want them even more. And just when you turn away, they're back. Your phone rings, a text pops up. The chase is on again.

I learned soon enough that this behavior was more than bad

manners. It was a bruising game of strategy. I didn't understand the rules, and after I'd had my feelings hurt a few times, I stopped caring. I gave up Italian men for Lent one year and never looked back.

So I was a bit wary of starting anything with Niccolò. During my sleepless night, I searched for him on Facebook and there he was. I scanned his friends list and under his last name, found a lovely girl in her late teens who looked to be his daughter and a guy holding a baby, who I assumed was Niccolò's son. I liked that Niccolò was a *nonno*, a grandpa, which made our age difference shrink a bit. His profile showed he was from Florence and that he now lived in a town nearby. Everything he had told me checked out.

Then I googled him. I didn't expect to find anything, but I was stunned to see a half dozen photos of him pop up above several links that featured him.

My Florence taxi driver had another life: He was a champion poker player.

He had won a hefty sum in a tournament several years earlier. I couldn't quite believe it was Niccolò. He was heavier then, which changed the shape of his face. I enlarged one photo and looked at the creases in his forehead, which matched the ones in his recent Facebook photos. This poker champ was indeed Niccolò.

I scanned the headings of the Google links and sat up straight when I saw an entry for him that said "MOB."

My god. Niccolò was a Mafia poker player, I thought. The writer-in-me grinned. *This could be fun*, she whispered. She always loved a good story populated by colorful characters.

I opened the Google link and realized MOB referred to the "Hendon Mob," four famous British poker players whose website provided the internet's largest poker database. I felt relieved, but intrigued.

I scrolled through photos of Niccolò. In one, at his big tournament win, he smiled at the camera with tall stacks of chips on the table in front of him alongside a silver trophy in the shape of a spade – as in the Ace of Spades. In another photo, from a tournament the following year, the caption read "*eliminato.*" His loss was painfully obvious, as he despondently stared into space.

I closed my iPad and stared at the ceiling. I would try to sleep. It was 5 a.m., too early to send Niccolò a message. I already knew what it would say: *So nice meeting you last evening. Hope to see you again soon.*

I sent that message later in the morning. My energy was flagging by early afternoon, so I lay down for a nap. I had just dozed off when my phone rang. It was Niccolò.

"Laura, it's Niccolò. Am I disturbing you?"

"No. I was just taking a nap."

"I'm so sorry. I don't know your habitude yet."

Habitude. A word from another era. That made me smile.

"It's okay. I usually don't take naps. But I didn't sleep well last night."

"I was wondering if you'd like to meet for coffee? Or would another day be better?"

"Today is fine."

"Are you sure?"

"Absolutely. I need to get some fresh air. When would you like to meet?"

"I'm working today, unfortunately. Are you working?"

I stifled a yawn. "Not today."

"I'll call you later, if that's okay."

After we said goodbye, I lay in bed for a few minutes, trying not to overthink what I was saying YES to.

Niccolò called back about 6:30 that evening. Actually, 6:30 is late afternoon in Italy. Italian dinnertime doesn't begin until 8 or later. The *aperitivo* hour begins around 6:30 or 7 when bars serve up drinks and hors d'oeuvres. The *aperitivo* habit is ingrained in Italian life. It's a breather at the end of the day, a way to ease into the evening over a glass of prosecco or a Spritz or something stronger. The coffee bars of Florence are well stocked with liquor and nibbles.

"I'll be on your street in five minutes," Niccolò said. "But I don't know if I'll find a place to park."

I suggested he go to the taxi stand at the bottom of my street, which had a small parking area.

"I can do that," he said. "Would you like me to come up to get you?"

We had decided to go to the Caffè Petrarca, which was across the street from the taxi stand. It was nice of him to offer to walk with me to the bar, but it would be quicker for me to meet him there.

"Wait for me at the bar. I'll be there in a few minutes."

"Whatever you prefer," he said.

Niccolò was at the entrance when I arrived. I almost didn't recognize him. He was wearing glasses and had cleaned up the scruff of his beard.

"Well, hello," I said, smiling at him. He was a bit taller than I, which was a nice surprise. At 5'7", I often find myself an inch or two taller than many Italian men.

"I'm happy to see you again," he said as we went up to the bar. "What would you like?"

"Prosecco would be nice."

Niccolò ordered my drink and an espresso for himself. "I'm working," he said to me. "No alcohol."

We sat down in the back room, where it was quiet, on opposite sides of a small table.

He looked at me for a moment in the bright light of the room and shook his head. "You look like you're 40."

I noticed he had put his glasses on the table. "Maybe you should put those back on," I said teasingly.

"I only need them for reading. Part of getting older." He studied my face. "You don't look like you didn't sleep last night."

"I've had a cold and haven't been sleeping well."

He clinked his cup with my glass. "To a good night's sleep then."

"This should help." I sipped my prosecco.

He glanced around the room. "So this is your bar?"

An often-asked question when you live in Florence is *what's your bar?* Your bar identifies your turf and the crowd you hang out with.

"It's named for a writer. A good bar for me."

Niccolò smiled. "I love how your eyes sparkle."

The seduction had begun. But I didn't feel Niccolò was about to pounce. He was doing what Italian men do. They caress a woman with their compliments and make her skin tingle with their eyes.

"Tell me what you're passionate about," he said.

I hesitated for a second as I contemplated my passions. I chose the ones suited to the moment. "I love traveling and writing about my experiences," I said simply.

"You are brave to do what you've done. To make a life far from your home. Why did you choose Italy?"

"I was a single mom for 13 years..."

"So you've been divorced for a long time?"

I nodded. It seemed like an eternity.

"In the summers, when my son spent time with his dad, I would come to Europe for a couple of weeks – on my own. I spent a lot of time in France. I thought that's where I'd end up. In Paris or maybe Provence."

"But here you are."

"Life has unexpected twists and turns," I said.

"*Si*. That I know."

I had told this story many times, but I still marveled that I had come through the trauma of it. "My son left for college in 2008, just before the global financial crisis began. I had planned to rent my house while I traveled for a year or two. But I saw what was coming, so I put my house up for sale that summer." I took a breath remembering the nightmare of that summer. "When it finally sold, I needed some time to figure out what next. On a whim, I booked a flight to Florence. I had visited Italy in college and thought it would be interesting to write a story about retracing my footsteps here – a woman at middle-age looking back at a journey she had taken in her youth."

I hadn't yet revealed my age to Niccolò. I think he would have been shocked to know that at the time of my college visit to Florence, he was 12 years old.

"I'm glad you're here." In that moment, I felt the pull of Niccolò's big heart.

"Tell me about you," I said. I could see him as a 12-year-old playing football with his pals. I wondered if I had walked past him in a Florence piazza one spring day in 1975.

Niccolò had taken the Classics tract in school, a difficult academic course in the Italian system that requires proficiency in Latin and Greek and focuses on literature and the sciences. He had learned English in school and studied philosophy.

"I am curious and have many interests," he told me. "I love music. When I was young, I used to translate lyrics from popular American songs. There was great music in the 70s."

I smiled. Of course, I knew the great music of the 70s.

Niccolò became a limo driver in the mid-1990s. "I worked 18 hours a day and had no life," he told me. "A few years ago, I needed to make a change."

I sensed he was recently divorced, but I didn't ask him about that. A few times while we were at the table, he checked his phone for messages. "When you have kids, you need to be available." I imagined Niccolò was a devoted father and son. His father was Florentine and his "mamma" came from northern Italy. With a finger, he drew a picture on the table showing me the valley in the mountains where she grew up.

The bar was getting ready to close. Unlike many Florence bars that stay open late, the Petrarca goes dark around 8. Niccolò paid our bill at the register and held open the door for me as we stepped outside.

I felt his hand at my back as we crossed the busy street. The Petrarca sits at a traffic circle outside an ancient gate of the city called Porta Romana that centuries ago had been the southern-most point of the immense wall that surrounded Florence. Most of the wall was torn down in modern times as the city expanded. But this towering 13th-century gate remains, its enormous wooden doors propped open to allow buses, cars and motorcycles a portal in and out of the Medieval Oltrarno district, where some of the tower houses and palazzos date back to the turn of the last millennium.

Despite my frustrations with daily life in Italy, I knew that the history and beauty of Florence fed my creative spirit. At some point, I was sure I would return to California. But at each juncture where I needed to assess the pros and cons of staying in Florence, I remained.

"Look," Niccolò said, pointing up at the moon.

It was full and bright, illuminating enormous puffy clouds that framed it.

"How beautiful," I said.

"Do you like a full moon?"

I had never been asked that before. But I knew in an instant the answer was yes.

I turned to Niccolò and told him the story of my former mother-in-law whose name was Lily.

"She was Italian – a war bride from Trieste."

"Really?"

"My father-in-law was an American GI stationed in Trieste during the Occupation. They married in Italy and he took her back to America." I smiled at Niccolò. "*That* took courage.

"On the night she died, there was a full moon. Every time I see one, I say hello to her." I could feel a catch in my throat as I looked up at the moon. "Hello, Lily," I whispered.

Niccolò stood quietly, looking at me. "What a beautiful story."

I noticed his cab across the street. I knew he had to get back to work, but he insisted on walking me home.

He said he had noticed that that my call the night before had come from the sports clinic. I explained I was being treated by a chiropractor for a sprained ankle.

"You seem to be walking fine," he said. "Are you okay now?"

"I'm much better. I just have to be careful on the cobbles."

"I have problems with my neck and work out with a personal trainer three times a week," he said.

"Were you in an accident?"

"No. I hurt my neck carrying luggage when I was a limo driver." He told me about his exercise and therapy regimen. "I'm working on my posture." He stopped in the middle of the sidewalk and threw back his shoulders. He seemed to grow two inches.

He tapped his chest, just below his collarbone. "Touch me here."

I flashed to a memory of my son when he was four years old, sprawled on a big beach towel that he shared with a darling five-year-old girl who lived across the street. They had just had a swim in a little splash pool in our backyard and were lounging in the shade when Kyle raised his arm and said to her, "Tickle me, right here." She tickled him and they both squealed with giggles.

I held out my hand to Niccolò and he pressed my fingers to the spot he wanted me to feel on his chest.

"That's muscle," he said proudly. He pronounced the "c" in muscle so it sounded like MUSKLE.

I looked at this Italian man, who wanted me to feel his "muskle," and thought, *Could you be any more adorable?*

When we reached the front gate of my apartment building, we made small talk for a few minutes.

"I'm so glad to know you, Niccolò." I finally said.

"Laura, truly the pleasure is all mine."

I gave him an air kiss on each cheek. He put an arm around me and I felt the warmth of his body under his puffer jacket.

"Aren't we lucky to meet by chance?" I said to him.

He smiled at me. "It was fate."

I opened the gate and turned back to look at him before I closed it. He stood on the sidewalk, under a Lily moon, grinning.

I blew him a little kiss.

Later that evening, I got a call from my English friend Abbie, who was one of my closest friends in Florence. She had been in her late 40s, living in London with her husband, when he died in a car crash several years ago. They had no children, so she pulled up stakes and came to Florence. "I thought I was going to die from grief," she once told me. "But Florence brought me back to life."

Abbie and I confided in each other about everything. She was a delightful redhead, full of spunk and beans.

I told her about Niccolò and she wanted to hear all the details. I gave her the highlights and said I'd fill her in the next evening. We had made plans to see the movie *La La Land* at Florence's grand old theater, The Odeon, where they show films in English.

But when we got to the theatre the next night, a woman got up in front of the stage and announced a screening of a Swedish art film. Forget about *La La Land*.

Abbie and I decided we didn't want to see a Swedish art film and went to the box office to get our money back. The woman at the ticket window said it wasn't possible to get a cash refund, even though *La La Land* had been advertised on the theater's website as the scheduled film that evening. She gave us a voucher for a free entry that we could use another time. A classic example of Italian customer disservice: Once a vendor has your money, you won't get it back no matter what the circumstances.

We went to the bar next door, where *aperitivo* was underway. But at this bar, it was *apericena* – a drink with a dinner buffet. We loaded our plates and made ourselves comfortable on cushy seats in the corner.

Abbie wanted to know all about Niccolò. "Have you heard from him today?" she asked.

"No."

"Why don't you text him?"

"I think it's his move."

"He bought you a drink, didn't he? A thank-you would be nice." Abbie had impeccable manners.

"I don't know what to say."

"Say you enjoyed seeing him," Abbie suggested.

I hate writing text messages. Mine usually tend to be 10 words or less. But for some odd reason, the text I started composing to Niccolò was morphing into a short story.

"What are you writing?" Abbie looked concerned.

"Nothing." I deleted the message. "I can't do this."

"Yes, you can. Try again."

"I *really* can't do this with you looking over my shoulder."

She looked away, but kept an eye on my progress and reviewed my succinct final draft: *Ciao Niccolò... so nice seeing you yesterday. Sogni d'oro. :)*

The Italian phrase I ended with means "sweet dreams" – literally, "dreams of gold." Abbie had spelled it for me.

"Send it," she urged.

My finger hovered over the screen. In fact, it hovered there for a good five minutes. I knew Abbie was tempted to grab the phone from me and end the agony.

I took a deep breath and clicked SEND.

"Let's see how many minutes it takes for him to reply. He's going to be so happy to hear from you." She squeezed my arm in her excitement.

My message had flown into the ether at 10:39 p.m. On a

Saturday night. My stomach tightened at the realization of what I had just done.

A few minutes passed without a response. "He's probably working and will text you back as soon as he can pull over," Abbie assured me.

"No," I said with certainty. "He's with someone. Oh my god. Why did I do this?"

"You did the right thing. You'll see."

We left the bar 15 minutes later. I got in a cab at the taxi stand around the corner, at Piazza della Repubblica. Niccolò wasn't in the queue.

I checked my phone when I got home. No reply.

Abbie called. "Have you heard anything?"

"No."

"He probably was in bed and fell back to sleep thinking of you."

"I don't think he's alone tonight." I wished more than anything I hadn't hit SEND.

Niccolò didn't reply until Monday afternoon. He didn't say much: *Buongiorno...hope to see you soon.*

I responded: *Hope you're having a good day. Ciao. xx*

Abbie called for an update and I read her the messages. "I've put this in neutral and that's where it's going to stay," I told her.

"I like the driving metaphor," she said. "You'll hear from him again."

I wasn't convinced.

She and I had planned to see *La La Land* that evening, but she had to work late. Abbie taught English at a university in Florence and was devoted to her students who sometimes needed her help after hours.

I desperately needed a diversion, so I decided to go to the movie alone. I called 4390 for a taxi. No chance of getting Niccolò. He worked for the other company.

That night, from the moment I gave my voucher to the Odeon's ticket-taker until the final credits rolled up the screen, I was in cinema heaven – back home in La La Land.

The L.A. locations made me homesick, especially when the film's lovers, Mia and Sebastian, strolled across the Colorado Street Bridge in Pasadena, where I had lived for many years. The music swept me away. And so did the story of the struggle of artists who put everything on the line to make their dreams come true. For years, I had immersed myself in L.A.'s movie culture, as I wrote film scripts that never sold. Truth was, I loved writing movie scripts even if they didn't sell. For years, during my career as a journalist, I was always constrained by the facts. What a joy it was to sit every day at my computer and bring the stories and characters of my imagination to life.

When I left the Odeon that night, I was humming Mia's song *The Fools Who Dream* and wanted to dance on Florence's Roman cobbles. I didn't give a thought to my pesky ankle.

I hummed all the way to my favorite pizzeria, La Bussola, around the corner from the theater. When I walked in the door, the waiters, who knew me well, greeted me with hugs and kisses.

I blame my *La La Land*-induced euphoria for what happened a few minutes later, as I settled in at a cozy table and took my first sip of wine.

I texted Niccolò.

When a hopeless romantic is in her element, there's no stopping her. I wrote: *Are you working tonight? I'm going to need a taxi home in about an hour...from the Odeon. No worries if you can't swing it.*

Twenty minutes later, he replied: *I'm working...but now I'm far away. Call me 10 min before.*

Abbie called a few minutes later. She shrieked with laughter when I told her what I had done.

"Call me the minute you get home," she said. "This is better than Netflix."

I savored every bite of my decadent pizza – white truffles with pecorino cheese – and fortified myself with a second glass of wine.

Before I left the restaurant, I went to the ladies room. I always carry a little toothbrush and paste for emergency dental hygiene. Breath freshened and lipstick applied, I went out into the night.

As I walked back to the Odeon, I texted Niccolò: *Ready when you are.*

My phone rang a few minutes later.

"Laura, where are you?"

I loved how Niccolò pronounced my name: *Lauw-ra*, with a rolled "r."

"I'm around the corner from the Odeon," I said.

"Okay. I'll see you in two minutes."

I was reading the fine print of one of the Odeon's movie posters when I heard a car racing down the street. I turned to see a taxi come around the corner.

Niccolò flipped on the dome light as I opened the front door.

"May I sit with you?" I asked.

He smiled. "Of course."

As soon as I got in and closed the door, he reached across and pulled the seat belt tight around me, latching the buckle. He clearly was a full-service taxi driver.

I looked at him and sighed. "I've seen the most wonderful movie tonight."

"I can tell," he said. "You look so happy."

"I am happy."

"Me, too."

We were halfway across Ponte alla Carraia, heading toward the Oltrarno, as I was telling Niccolò about the movie. He looked over at me and said, "Your smile is so beautiful." He waved his hand near his head. "I can't think straight when I look at you."

"Careful," I said. "Don't drive off the bridge."

Minutes later, we were on my street. He gave me a discount on the fare. I paid him and thanked him for the ride. As I leaned over to kiss his cheek, he gently turned my chin toward his and kissed me on the lips.

It was one of those kisses that starts gently and then takes your breath away. I closed my eyes and let it happen. I hadn't been kissed like that in a long time.

I pulled back and said good night. I opened the door and stepped out onto the street. But before I reached the sidewalk, Niccolò jumped out of the cab.

He was next to me in a second, his arms around my waist.

"Laura, I'm an Italian man." It sounded like an apology.

I stroked his cheek and smiled. "I've noticed that."

His lips were just a few inches from mine. He waited for me to kiss him. And I did.

His hands were suddenly under my top, pressing at the small of my back.

"You're a dangerous woman," he said. "I think you have some Irish in you."

"I do. There's definitely a red streak in me."

"*Passione*. I feel it."

If the old ladies on my street were peering through their shuttered windows that night, they no doubt were fanning themselves.

At one point, I could feel Niccolò's chest thumping as he kissed me.

"Your heart is pounding," I said to him.

"Now you're my doctor?"

"I'd like to be your nurse."

"Let's go upstairs," he whispered.

"Let's go slowly," I said.

"When can I see you again?"

"Tomorrow."

He sighed. "I have a problem tomorrow. I am divorced, as I told you. Tomorrow is my time to be with my daughter. I pick her up at 8 and she comes to my place for the night."

"Take her flowers," I said. "Tomorrow is Valentine's Day."

"It is?" He looked surprised. "I have an idea. I will drive around for a little while now and when it's midnight, I'll come back and give you a Valentine's kiss."

"You can give me one now."

Niccolò gladly gave me what I wanted.

As soon as I got upstairs, I texted Abbie: *Mamma mia!!!!!!!!!!!!!*

She called immediately. "Oh my god, oh my god," she kept saying as I told her how my *La La Land* evening had ended.

I fell asleep with a smile on my face. I woke up early – around 7 – and looked at my phone. Niccolò had texted me at 12:40 a.m. to say he had found a black glove in the taxi. *Could it be yours?*

I remembered taking my gloves off as I opened my handbag to pay the fare. I wondered if the other glove had fallen onto the street when I got out of the cab.

I put on some clothes and went downstairs. No stray glove. I texted Niccolò: *Good morning...I just realized I'm missing both gloves.*

A couple of hours later, he replied: *I found both.* I responded: *YAY! ;)*

These weren't ordinary gloves. They were Madova gloves, made of soft Italian leather and lined with cashmere. Madova is a well-known Florence glove maker that has been in business for most of the past century, except for a hiatus during World War II. Buying gloves at the Madova shop is a sublime experience that begins with placing your hand on a golden velvet cushion to determine your size. "Seven-and-a-half," the sales woman said to me on my first visit. "How do you know that?" I asked, mystified by the cushion method. She looked at me as if to say, "Trust me. We've been doing this for a 100 years." Gloves of every color fill the shelves that line the walls at Madova. So that customers can easily slip hand in glove, the sales staff uses wooden stretchers to coax open the gloves' fingers. Wrist-length gloves with cashmere lining cost around E50 (about $60) a pair – a very good price given the high quality of the materials and craftsmanship.

Understandably, I was relieved to know my Madovas were in good hands.

But this is where the story of Niccolò takes a perplexing turn.

He sent the message about the gloves on the morning of Valentine's Day, a Tuesday.

By Saturday, I hadn't heard from him. That night, I went out to dinner with Abbie and an Italian man she had been dating for several months, a cardiologist in his late 50s named Salvatore. An Italian friend of Salvatore's joined us – a guy in his 60s named Renzo, who was miserably married to a witchy woman who wouldn't give him a divorce. Although he still lived with his wife, Renzo wasn't constrained by the bonds of marriage and enjoyed an active social life without her.

Halfway through dinner, Abbie asked if I'd like to discuss my "dilemma" with our male dinner partners. The writer-in-me pulled out her steno pad.

Salvatore and Renzo listened attentively to my story of Niccolò and the gloves.

"I don't understand why he hasn't contacted me about returning them," I said.

Salvatore immediately understood why I was reluctant to take the initiative. "If you call him, he'll think you're after him and not the gloves."

"Exactly," I said.

"This is about strategy," he said.

Renzo was less inclined to strategize. He suggested I call the taxi company and tell them what happened.

"But that would be bad for Niccolò," Abbie said.

Renzo shrugged. "He's behaving badly."

Salvatore took another tack. "Send him a text saying you'd like him to the leave the gloves at the bar. That way, you don't have to see him if you don't want to."

Renzo and Abbie liked that idea.

"It feels like he's flipped the switch from on to off," I said. "Is this a game?"

"Women play the on-and-off game, too," Salvatore said.

"Is he waiting for me to make the next move?"

"Maybe," Salvatore said. "But don't do it."

Renzo agreed. "He's playing with you. If you had let him come up to your apartment the other night, you would have never seen him again."

"On a scale of one to ten, how would you rate Niccolò?" Abbie asked Renzo.

"Below zero," he said.

She turned to Salvatore. He looked at me empathetically and said, "I'd give him a two."

In that moment, I was sorry we'd had this conversation.

"What if he's been sick or had a family emergency?" I said.

Abbie nodded. "That's possible."

Renzo chuckled. "Maybe he's in the hospital with both of his hands in bandages so he can't use his phone."

Salvatore offered to check the patient lists when he made his rounds on Monday.

We all laughed. Renzo poured more wine.

"So what will you do, Laura?" Abbie asked.

"I won't call the taxi company," I said emphatically. "And I don't want to send him a message to leave the gloves at the bar – that seems harsh. Maybe I'll do nothing and see what happens."

"But don't you want your beautiful gloves back?" she asked.

"I do." I smiled at her. "But if the poor boy's hands are bandaged, I need to give him some time to return them."

Renzo chuckled and shook his head. "Americans."

"So how would an Italian woman handle this?" I asked him.

Renzo didn't have an answer to that. Neither did Salvatore, who said, "This is not black or white. There's gray in between."

HA! An Italian woman would cut off a man's balls to get her Madova gloves back.

I learned a lot from my coaching session with these two Italian men and was fascinated with their different points of view. Renzo seemed to have hardened his heart in his unhappy life. But Salvatore, the cardiologist, had a tender heart. I could tell he was caring and sensitive. I understood why Abbie had fallen in love with him.

After dinner, as the four of us stepped outside into the cold night air, Abbie put an arm around me. "Bet you wish you had your gloves."

"Actually, I have another pair." I reached into my handbag and pulled out my other Madovas, which were the color of aubergines.

I playfully waved them in the air and stepped toward the curb. "Taxi!"

Salvatore and Renzo burst out laughing.

I dreamed about gloves on golden cushions that night and woke up the next morning with a vision of Niccolò wrapped in bandages.

When Abbie called later that day, I told her the only message I wanted to send him was to ask if he was okay.

"Don't do it," she advised.

And then she told me something sweet. When the guys were paying the bill after our dinner, Renzo had said to Salvatore, "Laura is such a beautiful woman. How bad we are."

"What did he mean by that?" I asked her.

"He was saying how rude Italian men can be and that you deserve to be treated better."

"That was nice of him."

"And you know what Salvatore said?" I could hear the smile in Abbie's voice.

"What?"

"He said he's going to buy you a pair of gloves and introduce you to a really nice unmarried doctor."

I had a moment of clarity a couple of nights later. I was on a skype call with an expat friend who used to live in Florence.

After hearing the low scores Salvatore and Renzo had given Niccolò, she said, "I feel sorry for the guy. Give him a chance. You know how Italians are. They get caught up in the day-to-day chaos. Just send him a message saying you could meet him at the bar next time he's in the neighborhood. Keep it light. Be friendly."

So I sent Niccolò this friendly message: *Hi there...it seems we've both been busy. Hope all is well with you. I'm home all day tomorrow. If you're in the neighborhood, call me. We could meet at the Petrarca for coffee (and gloves).*

His reply made me laugh: *Sorry we have two days off for a strike.* A taxi strike. The perfect twist to this Italian tale.

He had signed off that message with a winky-smoochy face. I replied with a sad face next to a line of taxis.

The strike ended the next day. But a week went by without a word from him.

I reminded myself that I was dealing with a champion poker player. If he was holding onto the gloves thinking they'd keep me in the game, he was wrong.

Basta, I decided. Enough of Niccolò and the gloves. I was done.

~ 2 ~

First love

My mom called it "puppy love" when I fell head over heels for the first time.

I was 15, a sophomore in high school. I had a crush on a boy who was a year older than I, named Marc. He was smart and funny, with a great personality. An accomplished artist, he took classes like sculpting and jewelry making, offered at our progressive high school in the Chicago suburbs. He owned an impressive collection of antique pocket watches and always had one tucked in his jeans, tethered to a gold chain that hooked onto a belt loop.

The King of Hearts dance was coming up soon. It was a turnabout Valentine's Day dance – girls got to ask the guys. I wanted to ask him to the dance, but my stomach knotted up at the mere thought of popping that question.

I knew Marc through our church youth group. One snowy Saturday, a bunch of us went tobogganing. We had a couple of sleds and jumped on them at random, two or three of us at a time. I had just sat down at the front of one sled when suddenly Marc was behind me, pushing off. He held me tight as we went careening and screaming down the slope. We plowed into a drift at the bottom and rolled in the snow, laughing. By the time I had dusted myself off, with a playful hug from Marc, I was smitten.

He broke up with his girlfriend the following week. I wondered if that toboggan ride had had anything to do with it. Breakups at that age can happen for flimsier reasons.

Marc had a car and played the gracious chauffeur after our Sunday night Youth Fellowship meetings. We'd all pile in, sometimes sitting on each other's laps, as Marc made the rounds. A couple of weeks after the toboggan outing, he went a bit out of his way to drop off the others in the car, leaving me for last.

It was my big moment. The dance was in two weeks. I had heard from a friend of his that he hadn't been invited by anyone yet.

"I have something I'd like to ask you," I said, just as my stomach went into a twist.

"Sure."

I immediately lost my nerve. "Never mind. It's a stupid question."

"Ask me."

I had moved to the front seat after Julie and her brother Jeff had gotten out of the car. Marc turned to me. "Laura, what?"

"Nothing. Let's go."

He turned off the engine. "We're going to sit here until you ask your question."

It was a bitter cold night and it quickly got chilly inside the car. We sat there in the driveway for 15 minutes when finally Julie and Jeff's dad came out to see if Marc was having car trouble.

"No, Mr. Lawson. We're just having a fascinating conversation. Lovely night, isn't it?" Marc said.

Mr. Lawson shook his head and went back inside.

Marc rolled up the frosted window and looked at me, as I sat shivering.

"Laura," he said sweetly. He stretched himself across the front seat, with his head on my lap looking up at me. "You can ask me anything."

I took a deep breath. "I can't."

"Yes, you can."

I closed my eyes and summoned all the courage I could muster. Finally, I said, "Will you go to the dance with me?"

Marc sat up straight and started the car. As he turned to back out of the driveway, he smiled at me.

"Is that a yes?" I asked.

He leaned over and kissed me. "YESSSS."

I was euphoric. For the next two weeks, my life revolved around the King of Hearts dance. I got a new dress. I went to the florist and ordered a boutonniere for Marc – the first time I'd ever done that. Marc asked about the color of my dress so that he could order flowers for me as well.

Marc did things with a flourish. He didn't just order a lovely nosegay for me to carry at the dance. On the morning of Valentine's Day, a dozen long-stemmed red roses arrived.

My mother was thrilled. "Your first roses!" she exclaimed

when I opened the box. Watching her carefully put them in a vase, I had my first glimpse of my mom as a teenager, arranging bouquets from admirers. "We'll save one of these roses and press it," she told me. It was a mother-daughter moment that bridged a generation. Forty years later, when I cleaned out my parents' house, I found a hefty tome on a bookshelf in the living room and saw the yellowed edges of tissue paper protruding from the pages. I opened the book and smiled. There was one of Marc's roses my mother had saved for me. On the tissue she had written "Laura's first roses, from Marc" and the date.

Before the dance, my mother sat me down. Literally. She sat on my bed and I sat on the opposite twin bed. The "talk" went as follows:

"This is your first date," she said, smiling. "And that's wonderful."

I nodded, but sensed something not-totally-wonderful was coming.

"There's something you should know about boys."

The nascent writer-in-me scrambled for a pencil.

She looked at me sternly. "Don't let Marc kiss you on the first date."

I wondered if I should mention he had already kissed me, in the Lawson's driveway. But better judgment prevailed.

"If you let a boy kiss you on the first date, he'll have nothing to come back for."

My mother and I clearly had different definitions of *nothing*. The writer-in-me made a margin note.

She then presented me with a short list of rules:

- Marc must come to the door to pick me up. No honking from the curb.

- No sitting in the driveway when he brought me home.

- No calling boys! Marc must always call me.

My dad greeted Marc at the front door on the night of the dance. If Marc was nervous, he didn't show it as we posed for photos in the living room. My mom and giggling little sister sat on the couch as my dad snapped away. In my favorite photo from that night, Marc is beaming, hands behind his back, head cocked to one side. We look like the two happiest teenagers alive.

We had a wonderful time at the dance. Marc took me out to dinner afterward, to a little restaurant in town. He had promised he'd have me home by midnight and conscientiously kept an eye on the time – Marc was wearing a beautiful pocket watch that night.

The first months of our budding romance vaulted me into the clouds. I knew something was terribly wrong with my psycho-hormonal balance one day, when I absentmindedly put the phone book in the refrigerator.

Marc wasn't a typical teenage guy. He wasn't into sports and never attended school games. He was anti-establishment in his politics and very vocal in his opposition to the Vietnam War. It was 1970, when 18-year-olds could be drafted, but they weren't old enough to vote.

He had a streak of mischief and defiance that, at times, made me uneasy. He picked me up one night to go to the movies and told my parents he was taking me to see *Doctor Zhivago*. But when I got in the car, he said devilishly, "Want to go see *Easy Rider?*"

It was playing in a town nearby, but I felt uncomfortable that I'd either have to lie to my parents when they asked how I liked *Doctor Zhivago* or tell them we went to see a film that I knew they wouldn't approve of. We went to see *Doctor Zhivago* that night, but a couple of months later on another movie date, he took me to see *Midnight Cowboy*, which was rated X, and astonishingly was playing at the local theater. There was only one theater in our small town and the owner's daughter, who was in my high-school class, worked the ticket booth. She rolled her eyes at me when Marc produced fake IDs to get us into *Midnight Cowboy*. She knew we weren't 18, and the IDs were laughable.

But mostly, I loved being with Marc. He seemed much older and worldlier than most of the boys I knew. We'd take the train into Chicago to go to an art exhibition or a concert. He was well-read and a good writer. We passed notes to each other daily at school, between classes. His were a blend of poetry and prose, with sketches in the margins. He signed them "CYK," which meant *consider yourself kissed*.

My first feelings of sexual longing happened with Marc. He made me laugh once when he told me, "I don't have sexual dreams. I dream about gorgeous watches."

His passion for antique pocket watches took us to antique stores and watch repair shops. We went to a watch-and-clock auction one Saturday, and I assisted him as his scribe, recording each item's selling price in the program.

The undoing of Marc and me came with my realization that under his charismatic facade, he was insecure and wary of attachment. His family had moved many times, forcing him to acclimate to new places and make new friends to the point that he felt like he never belonged anywhere. The strain between us worsened. He started doing stupid things to make me jealous – flirting with other girls in our church group – or not calling for days on end that summer. I'd jump every time the phone rang, hoping it would be him. A tortured existence for a girl who wasn't allowed to call boys.

Marc had given me his class ring – going "steady" was popular then. But at the end of that summer, just six months after the King of Hearts dance, I gave the ring back. I could tell he was angry. "I don't want to play games," I told him. I was angry, too. But I also felt heartbroken.

Puppy love, my mother called it. But my relationship with Marc felt like so much more. He had changed my world.

During the next school year – my junior year, Marc's senior year – we'd sometimes pass in the halls. But we went out of our way to avoid each other. We ate in separate cafeterias. We didn't hang out in the same places.

But somehow we ended up in the same phys-ed dance class. One horrible day, we were doing a square dance involving two large concentric circles, with partners changing as the circles rotated. He was on the inner circle, moving toward me, as I stood on the outer. I prayed the music would stop before he reached me. No such luck. The dance involved holding your partner's hands. As he and I performed the dance steps, we never made eye contact. I don't know whose hands were sweating more – his or mine.

I didn't date much that year. I went out with friends mostly. My classes and extracurricular activities kept me busy. In the spring, I was on the May Queen court and needed an escort to the May dance ceremony. I asked the brother of one of my girlfriends to go with me. He was several years older and attended the college in town. He was like a big brother to me and was happy to be my date.

The May Court was announced on the Monday before the dance. Funny how I remember this so well. That night, Marc called to congratulate me.

I was stunned, but happy to hear from him.

"Are you free Friday night? I'd like to take you out," he said.

I was free, but I hesitated. "Marc, I already have a date to the dance. I've asked Tina's brother."

"That's ok. I didn't call about the dance. I want to see you," he said. "I miss you."

I worked part-time as a waitress at a steakhouse close to where I lived and was scheduled to work Friday night. I told Marc I'd see if I could get off early. In our exuberance, we didn't pin down the details of this date. He went to the steakhouse to pick me up at 8. But I had gotten off early and went home to freshen up.

I was ready and waiting at home at 8. I watched TV with my parents and sister and tried not to look at the clock on the mantel.

My mother looked as distressed as I felt. "Honey, what do you think has happened?"

"I don't know." It was 8:45. "I'm going upstairs and put on my pajamas."

I was halfway up the stairs, holding the banister, feeling like I could burst into tears, when the doorbell rang.

I opened the door and there Marc stood. "Sorry. I guess I should have been more specific about where I'd pick you up."

"Were you at the restaurant?"

"Yeah. I finally went in about 8:30 and they said you had left an hour ago."

"Wait just a sec," I told him. "Let me say goodbye to my folks."

I poked my head into the family room, where my parents and sister were still watching TV. "He's here. He thought he was picking me up from work." My mother looked relieved.

I grabbed my coat and got Marc out the door as fast as possible.

"You look nice," he said when we got in the car.

"I was on the verge of tears 10 minutes ago."

"Why?"

"I thought you weren't coming."

"Oh, Laura." He leaned over and kissed me.

We fell in love with each other that night. Real love, not puppy love.

Marc and I discovered how miserable we had been without each other, all the while pretending we were better off apart. There's something powerful that happens between two people, no matter how young or old, who have a second chance to fix a broken relationship that's worth fixing.

"I saw you at school on Monday, being photographed for the newspaper with the May Court," he told me that night. "I hated myself for having been such a jerk to you. If you tell me now you don't want to start up again, I'll accept that. But I want you to know how sorry I am."

It was then that I started to cry. Tears of happiness.

That night, I experienced happiness I had never known. I felt whole with Marc, like we were two intricately cut puzzle pieces that fit snugly together.

Then came the big surprise of the evening. Marc invited me to the prom. He had told me the previous year that he thought proms were a big waste of money, much to my disappointment. But he clearly had had a change of heart.

He spared no expense for prom night. My flowers were beautiful. He looked so handsome in his tux. After the dance, we went to a fancy hotel near Chicago's O'Hare Airport and dined on lobster and were served sorbet between courses. And then we did something crazy: We went to the airport and rode the escalators at the international terminal, in our prom attire. We had a little audience of world travelers and an airport janitor, applauding us, as we laughed ourselves silly. I think, even in the moment, we knew we were living a night of our lives that we could – or would – never repeat.

You don't realize, when you're young with your whole life ahead of you, how much your youth defines momentous events. I don't know at what age I crossed that line to a place where I felt older, a bit wiser, perhaps less inclined to ride airport escalators in party clothes just for the fun of it. Did it happen overnight or was it a gradual process? Did the candle blow out in a gust of wind or did the flame just slowly dwindle till the final flicker?

The summer before Marc left for college, we pretended a curtain wasn't about to come crashing down on us. He was going to a big state university about three hours away. I went with him to an orientation that summer and felt overwhelmed by the enormity of the campus. We were both being brave for different reasons: His world would be turning upside down again in a big way and my small world would feel very empty without him.

It was a heart-wrenching goodbye that September. We both cried.

"We'll get through this year," he assured me.

I wasn't sure if he thought I was going to apply to the same university so that we could be together. We hadn't discussed that yet. My parents were planning college visits that fall that would take us to Virginia, Massachusetts and California.

Part of me yearned to go far away, to really cut loose and be out in the world. I wanted to travel and spend a college year abroad. I knew Marc wanted to travel as well, so I hoped we could make that happen together.

Marc came home for a couple of weekend visits that fall. The first one was wonderful. I felt like nothing had shifted between us. But the second one, in late October, shook me to the core.

We had gone out that Saturday night for pizza with our friend Julie, who, along with her new boyfriend Terry, had hitched a ride home with Marc that weekend. All three of them lived in the same dorm and spent a lot of time together.

We came back to my house after dinner and were sitting in the living room, talking. Julie was telling me how she and Terry met when I overheard Terry quietly say to Marc, "Shit, that was funny the other day when Lynda's jeans unraveled. I knew if you kept picking at that seam long enough, you'd get your hand in her pants."

I looked at Marc incredulously, not believing what I had just heard.

Julie shot Terry a dirty look. "Jesus, Terry."

I calmly stood up and went into the kitchen. I leaned against the counter and closed my eyes.

"What the fuck?" I heard Marc say to Terry.

"I didn't mean for her to hear."

"God, you're such an ass."

I stood there for a minute, eyes shut, pretending it was just a bad dream. I heard Marc's footsteps in the hallway.

"Laura," he said quietly. "Look at me."

I opened my eyes. Marc stood on the opposite side of the counter. I could see the panic on his face.

"Lynda's a friend," he said. "The four of us are in a study group."

"It sounds like more than that, Marc. How is it that her jeans unraveled?"

"We sit together and..."

"What? You put your hand on her thigh and pick at the inseam of her jeans?"

"Laura..."

"Are you having sex with her?"

"No," he said adamantly.

"Don't lie to me, Marc."

"I'm not lying to you." I could hear the defiance in his voice.

My eyes burned, but I fought back the tears. I knew if he wasn't cheating on me yet, he probably would. And there was nothing I could do to stop that.

Marc came by the next day to say goodbye. Julie and Terry were waiting for him in the car, so we didn't have much time to talk.

He apologized for what had happened the night before.

"I love you, Laura. Nothing has changed."

For me, everything had changed. I essentially had taken myself out of circulation, my senior year in high school – the faithful girlfriend of a guy at college who, as it turns out, was having a great time picking apart the jeans of a girl in his study group.

I let Marc kiss me goodbye. But I felt strangely numb. I could tell he sensed that. He held me close, stroking my hair. "What are you thinking?" he asked.

The words were too painful to say. Marc's world wasn't mine anymore. And more than that, I knew then that our worlds would never be the same again.

"You should go," I said. "You have a long drive."

He looked stunned. I hadn't told him I loved him or assured him that things were okay between us.

He kissed me one last time. "I'll call you tonight."

"Okay. Be safe."

I watched from the porch as he walked to his car. He turned around to look at me. I could see that he was crying.

The high-school drama department was organizing a trip to London over the Christmas break. The itinerary sounded wonderful: West End theater; museum tours; side trips to Canterbury, Stratford-upon-Avon and Stonehenge; and New Year's Eve in Trafalgar Square.

For months, I had been depositing my waitress tips each week in a passbook savings account. The cost of the weeklong trip, including airfare and theater tickets, was incredibly cheap – something like $400 – but that seemed like a staggering amount to me then. On my Saturday afternoon shift at the steakhouse, I made about $20 in tips. It took many rolls of quarters to secure my spot on that trip to London, but I managed, and even had some spending money to spare.

A dozen of us had signed up for the trip. Most of us had been in English classes or school plays together, so we were a tight group from the start. As we gathered around a cafeteria table for the first trip meeting, I knew we were going to have a blast.

There was a guy in the group named Mark – with a "k" – who was a fantastic dancer, very athletic, and always landed roles in school musicals that allowed him to show off his muscular physique. I especially remember him as an Indian in a loincloth and, in another show, performing a ballet in tights.

Mark was a Casanova, who seemed to have a new girlfriend every few months. I didn't know him very well, but as our London group coalesced, he and I started hanging out together at lunchtime and during study periods.

Then one day, he asked me out. We went to a play at the local college. As we walked back to his car after the show, he took my hand.

"There's something I'd like to ask you," he said. "Are you still with Marc?"

"Yes and no."

"Could you elaborate on the yes part?"

"Yes, he calls me from school. I saw him a few weeks ago when he was home. But that didn't go well."

"What happened?"

"He's met someone. He says nothing has happened. Yet."

"Where does that leave you?"

"Good question."

"Could I help you answer that question?"

He stopped walking and turned to me, taking my other hand. "Will you give me a chance?"

Yes or no. A question that required a simple answer. I took a breath and could feel a weight lift from me as I said YES.

So this became the story of Marc and Mark.

For a few months, it was pretty much the story of Mark. He swept me away, excellent dancer that he was. He took me to our school Christmas Formal and I felt like Ginger Rogers as he twirled me around the dance floor. It was hard to make a false step with him – he was so good at moving my body with his.

Mark had the advantage of being the homeboy. But it was more than that. He was fun and full of surprises. He'd kidnap me after school and take me in his Rambler to the ice cream parlor in town. He'd leave little gifts for me in my locker: a silly card, my favorite chocolate or a book of poems he thought I'd like.

Mark didn't give me much of a chance to think about Marc, whose calls became more sporadic. I didn't hide from Marc what was happening. The night I told him that Mark and I were seeing each other, I thought the phone had gone dead. The silence lasted a full minute before he said goodbye. I felt bad for him in a way. But he had set this in motion and had only himself to blame.

By Christmastime, Marc had faded from my mind. All I could think about was the trip to London and sharing it with someone who was doing everything in his power to woo me.

As my Christmas gift to Mark, I bought us tickets to see *The Nutcracker* at the Arie Crown Theater in Chicago. All these years later, Mark and I still talk about that night. We had never before seen a theatrical production on that scale. The dancing and staging were extraordinary. I actually gasped when the parlor of Clara's house suddenly expanded into a set deep enough to occupy a 20-yard section of a football field. For both of us – two teens from a small town – our eyes opened to what the big city had to offer.

But that was just the beginning. Our trip to London was life-changing for both of us. We went to the theater every night. We saw Robert Morley in *How the Other Half Loves*, Diana Rigg in *Abelard and Heloise* and Alec Guinness in *Voyage Round My Father*. In years to come, I would be awed by many West End and Broadway shows with megastars such as Elizabeth Taylor, Jeremy Irons, Glenn Close and Benedict Cumberbatch. But the plays I saw on that first visit to London, as a 17-year-old, would always hold a special place in my heart because they marked the beginning of my love affair with the theater.

Our group stayed in host homes in and around London. My dear friend Katie and I were the guests of a lovely older woman named Mrs. Foster who lived in a village in Kent, about a half hour out of the city. I loved her cozy cottage, which had been her home since the 1930s. One night, she told Katie and me the story of spending the night in a fruit cellar at the back of the garden during a Blitz raid, with her young son who had a raging fever from the measles. It was a miracle they both had survived.

I fell in love with London and knew I would come back. I especially enjoyed experiencing it for the first time with Mark. London, for me, will always hold the romance of two infatuated teenagers. We weren't the only ones making out in the back of the bus. Two of our friends in the group fell in love on that trip and got married years later.

I remember a walk in the woods with Mark on a cold, foggy evening, at a park near Mrs. Foster's house. Mark kept a firm arm around me as we walked deeper into the woods. Everything was wet and mossy, shrouded in the mist. It seemed like we were alone in the world, where we could let our hearts take wing. As he kissed me, I truly felt weak in the knees. Mark, who could lift a lithe ballerina over his head, kept me upright.

A few nights later, the group was in Trafalgar Square watching Big Ben tick off the last minutes of the year. Mark and I stood on the steps outside the National Gallery as we greeted 1972, hugging each other as Big Ben's chimes and the shouts of revelers filled the night. I could imagine many New Year's Eves with Mark. If I were to name the Top Ten Nights of My Life, that definitely would be one of them.

We were both over the moon by the end of the trip. Sitting next to me on the plane, Mark kissed me as we made our descent to O'Hare. In just a few minutes, our escape from our normal high-school life would be over.

"Wow, that was a smooth landing," he said, smiling at me. "Three cheers to the pilot."

I looked out the window and started giggling.

"What's so funny," he asked, leaning over my shoulder to see out the window.

The plane was still a thousand feet off the ground.

The magic of London ended abruptly. We were back into the last two weeks of the semester. I barely saw Mark as I prepped for exams.

He kidnapped me one day after school and took me to the ice cream parlor.

"What's it going to be today?" he asked as we slipped into our favorite booth by the front window. "A peanut butter-and-chocolate banana split?"

"Oh, I don't know," I said, looking up at the menu board. "Maybe a strawberry soda."

"Cutting back?"

"After all those cream teas, my jeans are feeling a little tight."

Mark smiled at me. "It doesn't seem real, does it?"

"I keep wondering if it all was a dream."

Mark reached across the table and squeezed my hand. "*This* is real."

"I'm glad about that." I truly was.

He pulled a packet of photos out of his jacket pocket. "Look what I got."

"Our pictures!"

He patted the seat of the booth. "Come over here."

I slid beside him and tucked my arm through his.

Somewhere I still have a little photo album Mark made for me from that trip. He turned out to be a meticulous archivist of our pictures and mementos. Not long ago, he posted a photo on my Facebook page of me asleep, in the seat next to him, on the bus ride to Canterbury. He has a cute one of us at Stonehenge, pushing on opposite sides of a prehistoric monolith – it's no wonder those stones are now off limits to tourists. He took a sweet one of me holding a bouquet of flowers outside the Haymarket Theatre. My favorite is one of us, arms around each other, in Trafalgar Square on New Year's Eve, with Big Ben looming in the distance.

On the day that finals ended, Mark picked me up from school in his trusty Rambler. He had packed a picnic and took me out to a lake not far from town, where his parents had a little cabin. It wasn't winterized, so we quickly got a fire started and warmed ourselves as we toasted bread for sandwiches over the flames. We slathered our toast with mango chutney that Mark had brought back from London. What 17-year-old guy brings mango chutney back from London? Mark, as it turns out, was destined to become a gourmet chef.

We took a long walk around the lake and talked about where we might be in a year. He had applied to Illinois schools. I was casting my net wide and far.

He picked up a stone and skipped it across the water. "Do you see me in what you're dreaming about?" He asked that question with such tenderness.

"What I see is a little fuzzy at the moment." I took his hand. "Do you see me?"

"Absolutely."

We spent a lazy afternoon at the cabin. I fell asleep on the sofa listening to him read from a book of poetry he had found at a London bookstore. When I woke up an hour later, he was asleep beside me.

He stirred as I played with his curly hair. "This is the first time I've ever slept with a girl," he mumbled. "I like it."

It was getting dark as we packed up the Rambler to head home. We were both wiped out from finals week.

When we got to my house, he walked me to the back door.

"Want to go to a movie tomorrow night?" he asked.

"Our youth group is serving at a spaghetti supper at church tomorrow night."

"Maybe after?"

"Sounds good."

"Okay, I'll call you tomorrow." He gave me a hug.

I was barely in the backdoor, when my mom rushed into the kitchen. She was wide-eyed, which was unusual for my mom, who was always known for her unflappable poise.

"We have a problem," she said, looking to see if Mark was behind me. "He's not coming in, is he?"

"No, why? What's wrong?"

"Marc – you know, the *other* one – is in the living room."

"What?"

Just then, there was a knock at the backdoor. I could see Mark, holding one of my gloves.

"Don't invite him in." My mom stepped into the shadows of the kitchen as I opened the door.

"You dropped this," Mark said.

"Thanks."

"See you tomorrow."

My mother waited a moment, then quickly went over to the door and locked it with the security chain.

"What's Marc doing here?" I whispered.

"He wanted to surprise you."

I wasn't exactly thrilled. I could hear him talking to my dad in the living room and couldn't help but giggle. I couldn't imagine Marc was thrilled either.

"Where does he think I've been today?"

"I told him you went out with your girlfriends to celebrate. End of exams and all."

"Good thinking, Mom."

I popped into the powder room next to the kitchen to make sure I didn't look like I had just been sleeping on a sofa and steeled myself for whatever was to come.

I walked quietly down the hall, listening to my dad talk about the stock market, and appeared in the doorway of the living room. My dad stopped mid-sentence. "Well, look who's home."

I looked at Marc. "And look who's here. What a surprise."

Both Dad and Marc stood up. My dad quickly excused himself. "I'll let you two get re-acquainted." He was good at putting a fine point on things.

"I didn't see your car out front," I said to Marc.

"I walked over from Pastor B's house. It was a nice night and I thought a walk would do me good."

"You left your car there?"

"I'm staying there for a few days. It's winter break."

"Why aren't you at your parents'?"

"They moved – didn't you know?"

"No. When did this happen?"

"Before Christmas. They're in Florida now."

"It seems we have some catching up to do. Can I get you something to drink?"

"Sure."

"Your usual?"

He smiled. "That would be great."

"Make yourself comfortable. I'll be right back."

I cut through the dining room into the kitchen, where my mom, still wide-eyed, was sitting at the kitchen table with my dad.

"Honey, why is he here?" she asked.

"I haven't gotten to that part yet." I looked in the fridge. "Do we have any cherry cokes?"

"I think there are some in the pantry."

I made quick work of pouring the drinks and returning to Marc in the living room.

I sat down next to him on the sofa, at a safe distance. This wasn't going to be a fall-in-his-arms reunion.

"So..."

"What brings me here?" he said.

"We could start there."

"Well, I'm on break..." He took a swig of his coke. "Truth is, I wanted to see you."

I said nothing, not to be mean to him, but because I didn't know what to say.

"How was London?" he asked.

I could tell he was nervous, so I thought I should help him get to the reason for this surprise visit. "Marc, why are you here?"

"I needed to see you, Laura."

I could see he was struggling to keep himself in check. "Marc, what's wrong?"

"A lot of things." He cradled his head in his hands.

I gently stroked his back. "It's okay. You're here."

That weekend was a blur of confessions, heartache and tears.

That first night, as Marc and I sat in the living room, he was so distraught that I couldn't make sense of what was upsetting him.

It had started to snow, so I drove him back to Pastor B's house. He kept apologizing. "Could we talk tomorrow?" he asked.

"I work tomorrow. But I'll be helping at the church dinner tomorrow night. Maybe after?"

"Okay." He leaned over and kissed me on the forehead before he got out of the car.

I hardly slept that night. Mark called the next morning, asking what movie I'd like to see. "What time do you think you'll be done at the church?"

I couldn't lie to him. "I can't make it tonight." I told him what had happened after I got home. He listened and didn't say anything for a minute.

"I have no idea what's wrong," I said. "He's staying with Pastor B. I'm really glad about that."

"There are times, like now, when I think I couldn't love you more," Mark said.

"You're so sweet."

"Just know I'm thinking about you. Call me if you need anything. I mean that."

I worked the afternoon shift at the steakhouse and rushed home to change. When I got to the church, I saw Marc's car in the parking lot.

I could smell the spaghetti sauce cooking as I headed downstairs to Fellowship Hall. There was a gang of young cooks in the kitchen, buttering garlic bread and slicing salad veggies. Marc, in an apron, was at the stove, stirring the sauce.

I went over to him and gave him a little hug. "I see they've put you to work."

"Smells great, doesn't it?"

"I'm starved. Does the help get to eat first?"

"I think we can wangle you a plate," he said with a smile.

Marc seemed like himself. Everyone was happy to see him. I doubt if anyone, but Pastor B and me, could have guessed how much pain he was in that night.

All of us were busy for the next couple of hours, setting up, serving and clearing.

"I bet you're tired," Marc said to me as the dessert plates were being carried out to the tables.

"I've had a long day in waitress mode."

"C'mon. Let's go upstairs."

He led the way, up a creaky wooden staircase, to a hallway behind the sanctuary. He opened the door to Pastor B's study.

"He said we could talk here."

I followed him inside. There were logs and newspaper in the fireplace, ready to be lit.

"Did you do this?" I asked.

"Yeah." He took a box of matches off the mantel and crouched down at the hearth. He lit a match and held it to a wad of newspaper.

From where I sat on the sofa, I could see him in profile as the first flames lapped the logs. He stayed there for a minute, mesmerized by the fire.

Unlike the night before, he was calm and steady. I suspected Pastor B had helped with that.

Marc sat down beside me and began with a confession. He had lost his virginity to Lynda. No surprise there, I thought.

"My relationship with her was a mistake."

"Why do you say that?"

"Because I lost you as a result."

"Are you still seeing her?"

"No. It's over."

It was my turn to stare at the fire.

"I pretty much blew off classes last semester," Marc said. "I smoked a lot of weed. My grades suck. My dad and I have had a big blowup over it all. I won't be going to Florida anytime soon."

He reached over and took my hand.

"I have two things I want to say to you." He looked at me intently. "I will never love anyone the way I love you. And I'm so sorry I have given you good reason to doubt that. I hope you can forgive me."

I suddenly had a lump in my throat.

"The other thing..." He took a deep breath. "As you know, the draft lottery is Monday. If my number is low, I'm leaving."

"What do you mean?" But I knew exactly what he meant.

"I'm going to Canada. If I end up as draft bait, I'll leave." He squeezed my hand. "The consequence of this is pretty serious. I won't be able to come back. I don't know when I'll see my family again. Or you."

"Marc, don't do this."

"Laura, I won't get a deferment. My grades are shit." I could see the fear in his eyes. "I'm not going off to that fucking war."

In my charmed life until that moment, I had never personally had to face the consequence of a war. But heartrending war stories were part of my family's history. Two of my mother's brothers were missing in action at the same time during World War II. One was in the South Pacific. The other was pinned down for days in a swamp somewhere in Europe and came close to losing both of his legs. Weeks went by before the family knew if they were dead or alive. My mom, who was a teenager then, remembered going down into the basement one night to tend to the laundry and found her mother, who had been keeping a brave face, bent over the wash tub, sobbing. Fortunately, both of my uncles survived.

I didn't see Marc as a coward. In fact, I thought he was quite brave to stand by his convictions. He had voiced his opposition to the Vietnam War many times in spirited discussions with our friends, who also were facing the draft and feeling pressure from their fathers who had served in World War II or Korea.

Marc pulled me close to him. "What are you thinking?"

I lay my head on his shoulder and closed my eyes. I loved the sweet scent of him. It was a mix of bath soap and cologne.

"I will always love you, too." I had never felt such heartache.

We sat quietly watching the fire.

Marc drove me home. We parked in the driveway, enjoying a long good-night kiss – rules be damned.

The next morning, a Sunday, my parents laid down the law. Actually, it was my father who squared off with me.

I can still see him sitting in the big red-leather chair in the family room. It was my mother's favorite chair.

In an odd twist, he essentially took on her role in this matter. My mother would have been in no position to reprimand me. She had been the belle of every ball, with suitors lined up to whisk her around the dance floor.

My dad didn't mince words with me. "What happened here Friday night was unacceptable."

"Dad, I didn't know Marc would be here. We broke up a couple of months ago."

"But you were out with him last night."

"He wanted to talk to me."

"I don't want the details," my father said sternly. "You need to make a choice. Nice girls don't have a boyfriend at the back door and another one in the living room."

You need to make a choice. My father's words rang in my head the rest of the day.

Mark picked me up after lunch and took me to the lake. The sun was low in the sky and cast of puddle of yellow across the lake's surface.

It didn't seem possible that only two days earlier we had come here after finals and napped together on the sofa, without a care in the world.

Mark lit a fire and opened a thermos of hot chocolate he had made. He also had brought a packet of Walkers shortbread, another souvenir from London. I smiled as he put the finger-length cookies on a plate.

"This is homemade hot chocolate, I want you to know," he said, handing me a mug. "Not that Ovaltine crap."

We sank into the sofa and warmed our feet by the fire.

I cupped my hands around the steaming mug and savored the bittersweet taste. "Mmm, this is good."

"Glad you like it." Mark looked over at me. "So...the suspense is killing me. What happened last night?"

I laid my head back against the cushions and told him the story of Marc.

"He's serious about going to Canada?"

"His car is packed up. If his number is low, he'll leave tomorrow."

"How do you feel about this?"

"My heart hurts."

I didn't tell Mark about the choice my father had asked me to make. Part of me reasoned that the choice would be made for me if Marc drew a low number. He already had made up his mind to go. He had chosen his path. I couldn't change that.

But there was another part of me – the bleeding-heart romantic – that believed if I *chose* Marc, I could influence fate. I had this crazy idea that if I held onto him, by choice, he wouldn't get sucked away.

"Laura, are you still in love with him?"

"I don't know."

We sat in silence for a few minutes. Then Mark got up and threw another log on the fire. He put on his coat and quietly said, "I need some air."

When the door closed behind him, I started to cry. I knew that my irrational heart had chosen Marc.

The lottery results were broadcast over the radio the next day. The school newspaper staff posted the numbers and birthdates as they came in. I sat through an English class watching the wall clock tick off the minutes. When the bell rang, I raced down the hall to see the updated list.

A crowd had gathered in the hallway. One girl was in tears. Her brother had drawn a 10.

I frantically scanned the list and finally found Marc's birthday. His number: 304. I leaned against the wall, barely able to breathe.

"Is someone we know heading to Canada?"

Mark was at my side. I looked at him with sadness, even though my heart was pounding with relief and joy.

"No, he's ok. His number is high."

"Let go of this," Mark pleaded. "He's in no danger now. He can go back to school, to that girl he's been screwing. God, Laura. Why do you want him?"

"Mark, please..."

"I know this gave you a big scare. Were you thinking of going with him to Canada?"

"No."

"What then? Why all of a sudden do you want him and not me? We have something so much better than anything you could ever have with him. He was fooling around before you broke things off with him. He was going to leave the country without any concern for you. How can you possibly think he loves you?"

I couldn't look at Mark. I didn't want to hear this.

"I would never treat you the way he's treated you. Ever. Laura, we could be so happy together."

If I had really listened to Mark that day, I would have been a fool to do what I did next.

I gave him a kiss on the cheek and then walked away.

I went to my locker and grabbed my coat. Twenty minutes later, I opened the front gate at Pastor B's house, just as Marc opened the front door. He was down the porch steps in a leap and in two big strides, he had me in his arms.

We laughed and cried as we spun around together in the snow.

"I thought I was going to lose you," I said.

Marc kissed me hard. "You're never going to lose me again."

After the lottery, Marc went back to school. Mark and I broke up, and it wasn't long before he was dating other girls.

Marc and I went to Florida to visit his parents during spring break. The tension had eased between Marc and his dad. Marc had buckled down at school and was enjoying his classes that semester. Things were looking up.

Marc had been very attentive to me. He called me almost every night from school. We talked about me coming down for a weekend visit, but I knew my parents wouldn't approve.

The trip to Florida gave us a chance to hang out together. It was fun waking up down the hall from each other at his parents' house and having breakfast together in our pajamas. We made dinner together and stayed up late watching movies.

We took long walks on the beach and talked about everything, except for the one topic we really needed to discuss.

College acceptance letters would be arriving soon. I hadn't applied to Marc's school because I didn't want to go to a big state university. I was waiting to hear from several liberal-arts colleges, none of them close to home.

Marc had seemed okay with that. At least he hadn't voiced any objections. But I worried that our new tenuous feeling of commitment would rupture under the strain of a long-distance separation.

On our last day, we took a final walk on the beach. I was relishing the last hours of our time together, so it came as a jolt when Marc said, "Four more years of this seems like such a long time."

"Of what? Being apart, you mean?"

"Yeah."

"Are you having doubts?"

"Not doubts exactly." He put an arm around my shoulder. "I just see how hard this is going to be, with us so far away from each other."

"Especially when we know how good it can be when we're together."

"This has been a fun week." He kissed my cheek. "I have some good news. Pastor B has offered me a summer job. He needs some help with research for his doctoral thesis."

"Marc, that's wonderful! Will you stay with him?"

"Yeah." He smiled at me. "So you and I will get to spend the summer together."

A first step, I thought. I didn't want to think beyond that.

A few weeks after I got back from Florida, I was at the lunch table with friends who were talking about their plans for the prom.

Katie turned to me, "Is Marc coming home?"

"No, he's got a big art project he's working on at school."

Tina looked at me sympathetically. "You know my brother would love to take you."

"He was a great date to the May Dance," I said.

"Seriously, Laura, he'd jump at the chance to take you to the prom."

"It's an expensive evening."

"He's making good money."

"Marc wouldn't be happy."

"I hate to think of you missing out," Katie said.

"I'll be fine," I assured her.

As I walked down the hall after lunch, with prom posters plastered everywhere, I felt like I wasn't at the party – or the pre-party for that matter.

I stopped at my locker and found a note sticking out of my French book. It said: *If you don't have prom plans, could I be your date?*

I recognized the handwriting immediately. I turned around and saw Mark walking toward me.

"Are you spoken for?" he asked.

"Not for the prom."

"He's not coming home to take you?"

"No."

"Well then, will you go with me?"

"I thought you were seeing Kimberly."

"We went out a couple of times. I was just trying to make you jealous. But I didn't think you even noticed."

"I did."

"Really?" Mark grinned. "That makes me happy."

I laughed.

"Get your French book. I'll walk you to class," he said.

We turned a few heads on our way to my French class. I knew by the end of the afternoon the gossip in the halls would be that we were back together.

I was reminded that day of how much I liked Mark's easy-going nature and his take-the-world-by-the-tail confidence. I was also reminded of his great affection for me.

"So who's next on your list to ask to the prom?" I teased him.

"No one." He smiled. "My heart belongs to you."

On prom night, I was home with my mother and sister, popping popcorn for a movie night when the doorbell rang.

I was stunned when I opened the front door to see Mark, casually dressed, holding a lovely bouquet of spring flowers.

"I've come to whisk you away. You're not staying home on prom night. Not allowed."

I could hear my mother coming down the hallway to see who was at the door. Her eyes grew wide, this time at the sight of Mark with flowers.

"I'd like to take your daughter out for the evening, Mrs. Evans. May I have your permission?"

She turned to me. "Is it all right with you?"

That question hung in the air for a moment. What would I tell Marc – or should I tell him at all?

Mark instinctively solved my dilemma. "I'm here as your friend, to cheer you up on a night when you should be dancing with your prince at the ball."

I could feel my mom swoon a little. She squeezed my arm. "Go." And then she said, "It's a good thing your father is out of town."

Mark drove me to the cabin on the lake. He had packed a picnic supper, complete with candles and a tape player. After dinner, we slow danced on the deck, as Simon & Garfunkel and Gordon Lightfoot serenaded us under a canopy of stars.

Marc and I had a good summer. He loved the research he was doing for Pastor B and spent most of his days at the seminary library at the local college. He often came over in the evenings and had dinner with my family. My little sister, who was 10, adored him.

"I'm going to miss Marc so much when you go to college," she told me.

I laughed. "Are you going to miss me, too?"

"Well, yes. But he's really special."

I was going to a college 1,000 miles away. I wouldn't be home again until Christmas. I knew I would miss my family terribly. But my heart ached at the thought of being apart from Marc for that long.

One night, Marc and I went out for drive. We stopped at Dairy Queen and got Blizzard milkshakes. He took me to a secluded park by a stream that ran through town. We lay in the grass, which felt refreshingly cool. It had been a scorching hot day.

Marc rolled over on his side, next to me, and moved his hand up under my skirt. He slipped his fingers inside my pants. He had never done this before.

It was dark. There was no one around. I felt totally uninhibited.

Marc slowly brought me to a climax. At the peak of it, when I felt like I couldn't breathe, he whispered, "Just let it come."

He held me close, as I cried out. I felt like I was free-falling.

We lay on our bed of grass a long time, as he coaxed the last shudders out of me.

"Oh, Marc." That was all I could say.

"Your first time?" he asked.

I nodded.

"I'm glad it was with me," he said, smiling.

"Me, too."

On the day before I left for college, Marc picked me up early in the morning and took me out for breakfast.

"I know things are going to get crazy at your house, so I want to steal you away, just for an hour," he said, as he pulled into the IHOP parking lot. "Just you, me and pancakes."

We both ordered tall stacks. He liked his with blueberries. I slathered mine with butter and poured on the maple syrup. We had made pancakes every morning when we were in Florida at his parents' house.

I could see spending the rest of my life with Marc. We were very compatible and had many common interests. I wanted to travel with him. We had a long list of places we wanted to visit together. I could see having children with him someday. I wanted to grow old with him. I felt so sure our love would see us through anything.

At breakfast that morning, he presented me with a small box. Inside, nestled in lavender tissue, was a beautiful 1910 Baby Ben alarm clock.

He had written on a notecard tucked inside: *I give you this, for all the mornings I won't be with you to wake you myself.*

It was the start of a teary-eyed breakfast for me.

I reached across the table and held his hand. "I love you, Marc."

"I love you, too, Laura."

Marc and I started our separation with good intentions. We wrote to each other every day. We had long, expensive phone calls. He hitchhiked 1,000 miles to spend Thanksgiving with me.

I hadn't declared a major, but my interest was art history. I had a dynamic art-history professor who was the lead recruiter for a scholarship program at Oxford. He happened to be my academic adviser and suggested I apply. I discussed it with my parents over

Christmas break. I would essentially have a free ride except for travel and living expenses. They didn't want me to be so far away. But they knew, eventually, I would set off to see the world. I'd had wanderlust from an early age, as soon as I was old enough to curl up with a book.

Marc spent New Year's with us that year. We watched on TV as the ball dropped at Times Square in New York. I thought about the previous New Year's Eve in London with Mark. It truly seemed like it all had been an incredible dream.

I had bumped into Mark at a local bookstore just before Christmas. He looked well and asked if Marc and I were still together.

"If that ever changes, you'll let me know, won't you?" he said, giving me a peck on the cheek.

One morning, I came down to breakfast and found Marc at the kitchen table, looking at the Oxford packet I had brought home.

"What's this about?" he asked.

I poured myself some coffee. "My adviser has suggested I apply for an art-history scholarship there."

"In England?"

I nodded.

"When?"

"It would be a two-year program, starting next fall."

Marc looked at me as if I had just said I was going on a two-year mission to Mars. "You can't be serious."

"It's a wonderful opportunity – it's a full-ride scholarship. At Oxford."

Marc came unhinged in slow motion. *Wow* was all he said at

first. He was quiet for a moment, but I could see his anger rising.

He stared at me for a few seconds. "Have you any idea how difficult this past semester has been for me? I hitchhiked 2,000 miles round-trip just to spend Thanksgiving with you. And now you're telling me instead of being a mere 1,000 miles away, you're going to be 4,000 miles away with an ocean between us?"

"Marc, I've saved up some money. We can spend it on airfare. You can come see me and we'll travel together."

"No. This is crazy, Laura. You just keep raising the bar, expecting me to jump over it. You have no consideration for the toll all of this is taking on me. The truth is, you don't care, do you?"

"Of course, I care."

"Then stop this right now. All of this." He pushed back from the table and stood up. "Or I'm done. I swear to you I'm going to walk out of here and not look back."

I was too shocked to say anything for a minute. Everything hung in the balance – our relationship, our future together. But my future, my dreams were at stake, too.

I looked at him and said, "Then go." With two words, I tipped the scale.

He went upstairs and packed. A half hour later, Marc was gone.

Two-and-a-half years later, in May of 1975, I was back home for an interview at Northwestern University, north of Chicago, for a graduate program I was considering.

I got a call from Marc out of the blue. I don't know how he

knew I was home. He asked if I'd come down to see him. He had just graduated and had his apartment at school until August, when he'd be moving. He told me he had taken a job that started in September, teaching art at a high school in Peoria.

I spent a few days at his place. In spite of all that had happened, we had a great time together. We'd grown up. I was 20 and he was 21. Still so young, but more mature and a little wiser.

I thought back to when we were 15 and 16, on that night in the Lawson's driveway, with me falling apart over asking him to the King of Hearts dance. I understood for the first time the power of nostalgia, of reaching back to a time that you can't return to. Marc and I could never recapture our innocence with each other. But we had a wonderful memory of it.

For those few days, we lived a romance that might have lasted a lifetime. Marc couldn't have been a more loving lover and I happily gave myself to him.

One afternoon as we lay in bed, he asked about the program I was considering. There was no anger this time. He listened to my plans. I would finish up my undergraduate requirements at NU that summer and would begin a journalism program in the fall that would take me to New York City for a magazine internship during the spring quarter.

"It sounds great," he said, stroking my arm. "But I need to say something. I'm not going to follow you."

"So this is it?" I wasn't hurt or angry. In fact, I felt only love for him.

"No. Not necessarily. If you want me, you'll know where to find me. I'll be teaching high school in Peoria, Illinois."

He made it easy for me to walk away, and he knew that. I appreciated that he held his ground. I suspected he thought he might lose his footing if he didn't.

The next day, he drove me to the train that would take me back to Chicago. We stayed on the platform until the conductor's last whistle. We hugged and kissed. There were no words: No...*I love you.* Not even...*I'll call you.* We just held on tight to each other, as if gluing ourselves to that moment.

That was the last time I ever saw him.

One night the following winter, I sat on my bed at my NU student apartment, looking at the phone on my nightstand. I called information and got his number in Peoria. I dialed the first four digits, then hung up.

By the following summer, I had gotten a magazine job in New York City. The next Christmas I was home and saw a bunch of friends at a party in town. They were surprised I hadn't heard the news: Marc had gotten married a month earlier, to a woman who was also a teacher at Peoria High School.

Later that night, as I turned down the street where my parents lived, I pulled over for a few minutes to catch my breath. I felt like the wind had been knocked out of me. A chapter of my life had ended. My first love was married.

And two years after that, Mark was married, too.

~3~

Betrayal

I didn't marry until I was 32.

My high school and college friends had almost given up on seeing me walk down the aisle despite the fact that, in my decade as a single woman with a closet full of bridesmaid's dresses, I had an impressive record of catching bridal bouquets. At one friend's wedding, I leapt a foot in the air, in stilettos, and made a spectacular grab that prompted one handsome guest to hand me his card. "I'm a scout for the Yankees," he said. "We could use you in the outfield."

I've often wondered what happened to that guy. I blew him off, but later regretted that. He had the best pick-up line ever.

I met my future husband when I was living in Manhattan. Ryan worked in the same building, on the same floor. I marveled at how often we ended up riding the elevator together. But he later confessed that he had asked his secretary, who had a view of the corridor, to buzz him whenever she saw me leave the office.

We weren't a perfect fit, Ryan and I. In fact, we weren't at all alike. He would rather go to a boxing match than a Broadway play.

He loved to hike and camp in the wild. My idea of a good time was sunning myself at a swim-up bar, sipping an umbrella drink. He was Mr. Math & Science. I was Ms. Arts & Humanities. He was a Republican. I purposefully cast a vote against his in every election of our married life.

We didn't rush into marriage. We dated for a couple of years and had a good time together. But neither of us was inclined to commit. We were both wedded to our careers at that point. Ryan was an architect at a big international firm and traveled a fair amount, which gave me some breathing room. We each had our own apartments on the Upper West Side, which in those days, was still semi-affordable.

Our pseudo-detachment left the door open to a love affair that would become the biggest WHAT IF of my life.

My first encounter with Gavin was at the opening of a major exhibit he had curated at the Museum of Modern Art in New York, in 1985. I was working for an arts magazine then and had been assigned to write a profile about him. Gavin was English and had made a name for himself in London, but the MoMA show had secured his status as one of the top contemporary-art curators in the world.

I'll always remember the night of the opening, watching him work the room. Actually, the room came to him. He seemed to stand head-and-shoulders above everyone – his tousled, dark, wavy hair catching the light. There was something magnetic about Gavin. He used his British charm and wit to good advantage. But it was more than that. There was a riveting intensity about him that I found very seductive.

We had arranged to meet for lunch two days later, at a quiet bistro in Greenwich Village. He had arrived early and gotten a table out on the back patio. It was a beautiful spring day. A bower of blooming wisteria hung from a pergola above the patio. As I sat down next to him, a slight breeze created a shower of purple petals that dressed our table and clung to my auburn curls.

"Incredible," Gavin said. "How did you manage that?"

He told me later that I took his breath away that day – the woman with wisteria petals in her hair.

Our lunch lasted three hours. Sometime after the waiter uncorked the second bottle of wine, I stopped thinking about my interview questions and enjoyed letting our conversation wander.

We discovered that Gavin's best friend had been a classmate of mine at Oxford, which sent us down cobbled streets and back alleys to places we had in common. It was quite possible, back then, that we had been at the same gallery or the same pub at the same time.

Gavin invited me to join him for a gallery reception the next evening. I told myself it was necessary research for my article, and that turned out to be partly true. Gavin graciously introduced me to the well-heeled art patrons at the party. It seemed he knew everyone. I added many names to my Rolodex that evening.

Afterward, Gavin took me to a jazz club nearby. We sat at the bar and he ordered two glasses of expensive Scotch.

"Something to remind you of your days in Britain," he said.

I laughed, as we clinked glasses. "*This* was way out of my league. I was doing pints of cheap ale back then."

As the Scotch warmed me, I knew I would end up in bed with Gavin that night.

We went back to his place. He was staying at a townhouse on the Upper East Side, provided for his use by a MoMA benefactor, that looked like something out of *Architectural Digest*. The art collection alone was worth millions.

But we didn't linger over the art that night. Gavin quickly led me to the bedroom.

"I haven't asked you if you're a free woman," he said, unzipping my dress.

Thoughts of Ryan hadn't crossed my mind all evening. I let my dress fall to the floor and smiled. "I'm yours."

For the next two weeks, Gavin and I were inseparable. Ryan was in Italy, finalizing plans for a concert hall he was working on in Milan. Skype hadn't been invented yet and international calls were prohibitively expensive. So I had a blissful hiatus from a relationship that paled in comparison to what I was experiencing with Gavin.

One night, Gavin came over to my place for dinner and saw a photo of Ryan and me that I had forgotten to put away.

Gavin wasn't angry or surprised. "Are you in love with him?" he asked.

I didn't hesitate for a moment. "No, I'm not."

"Good," Gavin said. "What will you do when he comes back?"

"That depends."

"On what?"

"On you."

He took me in his arms and kissed me. "I like that answer."

The day Ryan returned from Italy, I had been out to lunch with Gavin. I walked into my office to see a vase of roses on my desk. The card read: *How I've missed you.*

Ryan appeared at my office a few hours later. I was on a call as he tapped on the open door. I knew immediately I was in trouble when my heart didn't leap at the sight of him.

Despite his jet lag, Ryan took me out to dinner that night. He was struggling to stay awake when we came back to my apartment. Our lovemaking that night left me feeling empty. I was awake long after Ryan fell asleep, undone by the mess I was in.

Gavin called me at work the next day. I knew there was something wrong the moment I heard his voice. "I need to see you," he said. "Now."

"Where are you?"

"At home. Can you get away for an hour?"

"Sure. I'll grab a cab and be right over."

Gavin greeted me in his bathrobe. He was unshaven and looked like he hadn't slept. I could smell Scotch on his breath.

He didn't need to tell me what was wrong. I knew.

"Tell me you want me, Laura."

"I want you..."

I barely got the words out before his mouth was on mine. I could feel the burn of his jealousy and desire.

Gavin had one intention that day – to erase Ryan from my thoughts, my heart, my life. He took me to his bed, wanting to give me pleasure I had never known. *Tell me what you want,* he whispered over and over as we made love. I had never felt such ravenous sexual hunger and Gavin delighted in whetting my appetite.

I didn't go back to work that day. I called in to say I wasn't feeling well. But I didn't call Ryan. I couldn't bring myself to tell him *that* little lie when I had a brutal betrayal to confess.

As twilight crept in through the bedroom windows, I felt safely cocooned in my secret world with Gavin. For that night, he was all I cared about.

The next day was a Saturday. Gavin and I slept in and when I called home mid-morning to check my answering machine – there were no cell phones then – I had a slew of messages, all from Ryan. The last one had been an hour earlier. *God, Laura, I'm so worried about you...* I couldn't listen to the rest.

I was sitting with Gavin at his kitchen table as I hung up the phone.

"How many messages?" he asked.

"Ten."

"Christ. Did he call the police?"

"He didn't mention that."

"What are you going to do?"

"I need to tell him."

Gavin got up from the table and poured himself another cup of coffee. I can still see him leaning against the kitchen counter with the sun streaming in the window behind him. His face was in shadow, which didn't give me warning of what was coming.

"Laura, you need to know something."

"What?"

"I'm engaged."

I was too stunned to say anything for a minute. He came back to the table and sat down next to me. He reached out to put his hand on my arm, but I instantly pulled away.

"I'm sorry I didn't tell you sooner."

"You're *sorry*?" I looked at him incredulously. "How could you lead me on like this?"

"Laura, I've been thinking a lot about..."

"About how I've stupidly believed your bullshit? *I need you, Laura. Tell me you want me, Laura.*"

"This is not what you think..."

I stormed out of the kitchen and was in the bedroom getting dressed when he appeared in the doorway.

"Laura, please hear me out."

I turned to him, my eyes stinging. "So this was just a little pre-marital fling?"

"I've decided to break off the engagement," he said. "It's you I want."

"When did you *decide* this?"

"I've been having second thoughts for a while. But meeting you convinced me I can't marry Isabelle."

Isabelle. I didn't know it then, but Isabelle – a woman I would never meet – in fact, would become a phantom in my life.

"What are you saying, Gavin?"

Neither of us moved toward each other. We both seemed rooted on opposite sides of a chasm that had suddenly opened between us – Gavin standing in the doorway and me, in my bra and panties, sitting on the edge of his bed.

I felt more heartache than joy when he said, "I'm falling in love with you."

I called Ryan later that afternoon. He was both relieved to hear from me and angry that I had caused him so much worry. I couldn't face going home that day and having him appear at my door. So I stayed another night with Gavin, who did everything in his power to soothe me.

The next day, I met Ryan for brunch and didn't wait until dessert to break the news. After a few sips of a potent Bloody Mary, I said, "I've met someone."

It took a few seconds for this to register with Ryan, whose belief system about me didn't allow for the possibility of someone who could tempt me.

His first question: "Are you having sex with him?"

"Yes, I am."

"Do you love him?"

I was annoyed that he had put sex before love on his list of concerns.

"It's still early days. But yes, I think I'm falling in love."

Ryan pulled his napkin from his lap and slammed it on the table. "You expect me to enjoy a meal after that opening?"

I said nothing. It seemed pointless to apologize for spoiling his brunch.

Ryan left in a huff, stumbling over the leg of a chair on his way out. I canceled his order, but stayed for my eggs Benedict. I was starving.

I took a long walk after I left the restaurant, feeling happily numb after a second Bloody Mary. I was glad to have made my confession to Ryan. But I hadn't begun to comprehend the drama I was being sucked into with Gavin.

Gavin had been engaged to Isabelle for a few months, but they hadn't set a date yet. Isabelle, who lived in London, had agreed to put off wedding planning until Gavin returned from the MoMA show.

His crisis involved more than Isabelle and me. MoMA had offered him a full-time position, which he wanted to accept. But he knew Isabelle would never leave London.

Gavin and I had stayed up half the previous night discussing what to do. "I have to end this with her. The sooner, the better," he told me. "I'm so sorry to put you through this."

When I returned to his apartment that afternoon, he had already booked his ticket to London. He would be leaving in a few days and would be back in a couple of weeks.

Gavin was upbeat and eager to start his new life in New York with me. For those few days before he left, we were incredibly happy.

It felt almost too good to be true.

I had some vacation time coming and desperately needed to get out of town. While Gavin was away, I decided it would be good to go home and spend a week with my parents. A well-timed visit, I thought. My parents would be celebrating their 35th wedding anniversary.

They still lived in the same house in the Chicago suburbs, though each time I came home the house seemed to shrink a little. In fact, everything in my little hometown seemed smaller. Living in Manhattan clearly had distorted my perspective.

My father had recently had back surgery and spent a lot of time during my visit stretched out on the sofa in the family room. The first night I was home, he was doing leg stretches on the sofa and my mom was knitting, in her favorite red-leather chair, when she asked, "How's Ryan? We hoped he'd be coming with you this trip."

My parents loved Ryan. He was the son they never had. I knew if we ever broke up, I wouldn't get much sympathy from them. I braced myself for that.

I sunk a little deeper into the overstuffed chair I was sitting on and grabbed a throw pillow for protection. "I've fallen in love with someone else," I said matter-of-factly.

It would have been much easier to say *we've broken up* or *we've decided to spend some time apart* and then fuzz up the details. But why bury the lede? The screaming headline was that I was in love with Gavin.

Predictably, my mom's eyes widened in disbelief. My father froze for a moment, holding a knee to his chest.

"You've broken up with Ryan?" My mother dropped her knitting needles on her lap.

"Yes. It's over."

"Honey, what happened? Who is this new person?"

"His name is Gavin. He's an art curator from London who has a big show in New York right now. I was assigned to write an article about him and...it happened."

"This is so sudden," my dad said, gingerly lowering his leg. "How long have you known this guy?"

"Not long. Just a few weeks."

"Don't you think it's too soon to know if you're in love?" he asked.

"Maybe. But we won't know unless we give ourselves a chance to find out."

Mom looked like she was on the verge of tears. "What about poor Ryan? Does he know?"

"Yes, I've told him."

"He must be heartbroken." She put a hand on her chest. "I'm heartbroken. I know it's selfish of me to say that. I'm sorry. It's just that your father and I thought Ryan was perfect for you. You seemed so happy together."

"Nothing horrible happened between us. Ryan is a great guy."

"Does this mean you'll be moving to London?" my dad asked.

I made a wise decision in that moment not to tell them about Gavin's engagement. "No. Gavin has been offered a job in New York, at the Museum of Modern Art."

"Well, at least that's *some* good news." Dad sat up slowly and swung his feet onto the floor. In a classic Dad moment, he looked at my mother and me and said, "What do you say we go out for a Dairy Queen?"

Later that night, I sat out on the screened-in back porch, rocking on the glider and sipping my Blizzard milkshake. I watched lightning bugs flash and saw myself as a kid running around the yard trying to snatch them out of the air. My dad would punch holes with a screwdriver in the lid of a glass jar, where I would lower my captives onto a bed of grass blades – their new home – for what always turned out to be the last night of their lives.

In years to come, when I'd bring Kyle to visit my parents at this house, I broke with that tradition. I showed him how to gently scoop lightning bugs into his hands. Growing up in California, he had never seen lightning bugs before. They were magical, out-of-this-world creatures to him. He loved watching them glow in his little hand-cave and laughed at the tickle he'd feel as they crawled on his skin. And when I'd tell him they needed to go home to their families and sleep in their own beds, he'd happily release them, sending them off into the night with a puff of his breath. A lesson in not loving nature to death.

I slurped the last of my Blizzard. The porch door creaked as Mom appeared.

"May I join you?" she asked.

"Sure." I wasn't so sure I could take another Q&A session that night about my tortured love life. But to my surprise, Mom didn't go there.

It was getting dark. She sat down next to me and lit a candle on the table next to us. She looked lovely in the candlelight. It was one of those moments when I could plainly see her in her youth.

In the story she told me that night, she was a young married woman.

"I've never shared this with anyone," she said. "It's been a secret I've kept for a long time." She reached over and squeezed my hand. "Your father and I had been married for a couple of years..."

They were living in the town where she grew up, in southern Illinois, back then. Although my dad was from a town only ten miles away, they didn't meet each other until they were in college, in the late 1940s. He always said he fell for her the first time he saw her – which made me discount his question to me earlier that evening about how I knew so soon that I was in love with Gavin.

"I had a boyfriend named Lewis when I was in high school," she said. "You've heard me speak of him."

I had heard many stories about Lewis. He was the original All-American guy. Smart, athletic, handsome, charismatic, the most likely to succeed. In their high-school yearbook, Mom and Lewis were named Best-Looking Couple. They were everywhere in that yearbook. He was Class President and the captain of the basketball team. She was the school's newspaper editor and the star of the Senior play. My favorite photo of them is at Mom's May Queen coronation, with Lewis escorting her across the football field to her throne on a festooned stage. Mom, in her billowing gown, looks like a Hollywood starlet, and dashing Lewis, with his elbow tightly crooked around her gloved hand, looks like the happiest guy on earth.

"I was in love with Lewis before I met your father. When I went away to college, Lewis and I wrote to each other every day. I had his picture on my dresser..."

I smiled, knowing what was coming next.

"You know, your father had a fraternity brother sneak into my dorm room one day when I was out and steal Lewis' photo. Can you imagine that?"

I laughed. "He didn't want Lewis lurking in your bedroom."

"Your father was so jealous of Lewis, which made what happened so awful for me." She hesitated for a moment. "I'll never forget the day I heard the news. Lewis was working in Springfield then. He had just gotten out of law school and was clerking for a state judge. I'd see his mom at the grocery store every so often and she'd tell me what he was doing. But on this one particular day, she hugged me and started to cry. Lewis had been diagnosed with Hodgkin's lymphoma."

I knew that part of the story, too. It broke my heart every time I heard Mom tell it.

"He came home and stayed with his parents for a while, but he got so sick he had to go into the hospital. There was no treatment they could give him in those days. He suffered horribly..."

In the candle glow, I could see the tears in her eyes.

"I wanted to go see him, but I felt I shouldn't. I was *married.* I didn't want to upset your father. But it became unbearable... Lewis was dying and wanted to see me. He begged our friends, who were visiting him at the hospital, to get me to come. They all were so angry with me and kept saying, *How can you not go to him? How can you be so heartless?*

"One night, when your father was away on a business trip, I waited until after visiting hours and drove to the hospital, by myself. I had called ahead to find out what room Lewis was in. I went in through a side entrance and remember going up a dark stairwell and tiptoeing down the hallway. I was terrified of getting caught. I think an angel must have been with me that night.

"I slipped into the room and closed the door. Lewis was asleep. I was grateful for that. I was shocked to see the state he was in. He was so gaunt and frail. I sat beside the bed, and when I touched his hand, he opened his eyes. *I'm here Lewis,* I whispered. He smiled at me and said, *I knew you would come.*

"I took off my coat and shoes and got in bed beside him. We kissed. Gentle, little kisses. He told me how much he loved me. And I told him I loved him, too. I truly did love him."

Mom held my hand tight. I felt fused with her, as if her secret were passing from her veins into mine.

"All these years later, I still wonder..." Her voice broke as she started to cry.

I almost couldn't bear to hear what she was about to say. *If she had chosen Lewis...*

"If I had married Lewis instead of your father..."

"Mom, don't do this."

"I loved them both. Did I unknowingly choose the stronger one? If I had chosen Lewis...would he have lived?"

She looked at me as if I had the answer. I put my arms around her and hugged her. "Mom, what happened to Lewis is not your fault."

I cried with her as we sat rocking on the glider that night. I had never felt closer to her.

She told me about how she sobbed at Lewis' funeral, with my dad sitting stoically at her side. She said everyone thought she was crying out of guilt for not going to see Lewis before he died. No one knew she cried for lost love.

And to think she kept that secret for 33 years.

A few days later, my mother and father celebrated their 35th wedding anniversary. The three of us went out to dinner. The waiter served a cake I had made for them. My gift to them was a photo I had framed from their wedding day. It shows them leaving my grandparents' house, in a shower of rice, as guests waved goodbye. The photographer has captured, in one brilliant click, my mother losing her footing on the steps of the front walkway leading to the street. You see the surprise on her face as she starts to fall. My strapping, sure-footed father has his outstretched arm around her waist, with a grin on his face that says *I've got you.*

"Your first act of gallantry as a married man." Mom leaned over and kissed Dad's cheek. "Thank you, darling."

"My pleasure." Dad smiled as he looked at the photo. He was the strong one who had won her in the end.

I went back to New York a few days later. My answering machine was full of messages, most of them from Ryan. I hadn't told him I was going home to see my parents. He probably thought I was away with Gavin. I didn't think I needed to explain my absence or whereabouts. We were no longer a couple. I could hear exasperation in his voice, but mostly I heard his misery.

The last message on the machine was from Gavin, calling from London to tell me he was coming back early. In fact, he'd be in New York later that afternoon.

My doorbell rang around 7. He had come straight from the airport, with his suitcase and briefcase in tow.

I didn't sense that anything was amiss. He lifted me a few inches off the floor as he hugged me. "God, I've missed you," he said.

He opened his briefcase and pulled out a bottle of duty-free Glenfiddich.

I smiled at him. "Nice."

As I reached up into the kitchen cupboard to get the glasses, he stood behind me with his arms around me. He nuzzled my neck. "I've missed the scent of you."

"What scent is that exactly?"

"Hmm...a delicate blend of wisteria petals and Scotch."

I laughed. "I haven't had a drop of Scotch since I last saw you."

"In my memory of you, I'll always think of wisteria and that single-malt perfume you wore on our first night together." He kissed my cheek.

I poured our drinks and we sat down on the sofa.

I held up my glass. "Do we have reason to celebrate?"

He looked at me with such sadness.

"Gavin, what's wrong?"

The Scotch numbed some of the pain for us both that night as Gavin told me what had happened with Isabelle.

"I saw her the first night I got back," he said. "We met for dinner at our favorite restaurant. She came straight from work, with a binder in her briefcase."

"A binder?"

"Yeah. Full of wedding stuff. Price quotes from caterers and florists. She'd already decided on a church and was working on a guest list." Gavin leaned back against the sofa cushion. "I said I thought we had agreed to wait and do this together. But she said she was excited and wanted to get a jump on things.

"When we got back to her place after dinner, I told her I was having second thoughts. She went crazy. I mean really crazy. She started shouting at me. *You met someone, didn't you? Who is she?* She took off her engagement ring and threw it at me. *Why don't you give this to her?* I left the ring on the floor and walked out."

Gavin rubbed the bridge of his nose. "I've had a splitting headache ever since."

"That wasn't the end of it?"

"I wish. Two days later, she called and asked if we could meet for coffee. When I saw her, she had the ring back on her finger. I told her that I had been offered a job at MoMA and wanted to move to New York. She said that was out of the question, which is what I knew she would say. I said I was really sorry, but I wanted to break off the engagement. She opened her handbag – god, for a minute I thought she had a gun – and she pulled out one of those pregnancy-test sticks and slid it across the table. Suddenly, I understood the rush to get married."

"She's pregnant?"

Gavin nodded. "About seven weeks."

"What will you do?"

"Laura, how can I walk away? I'm going to be a father."

The night Gavin made his big revelation marked an important threshold in my life. Once I stepped over it, I began to look at love differently. In my relationship with Gavin, I had seen the dark side of love. Just knowing that love had a dark side made me more cautious and wary.

As Gavin and I made love for the last time, in the haze of duty-free Scotch, passion gave way to pain that spilled into a bottomless pit of grief. I cried myself to sleep that night. This wasn't what love was supposed to feel like. I cried not only because I was losing Gavin, but also because my heart has lost its romantic innocence.

Gavin was gone when I woke up the next morning. He had left a note by the bed: *I will always love you.*

As bad luck would have it, when I arrived for work that morning, Ryan was in the lobby, waiting at the elevators. Before I could lose myself in the crowd, I knew he had seen me. He maneuvered his way toward me and got on the same car.

Ryan stood next to me, but we didn't speak until we got off at our floor.

I felt like crap and looked like hell. My eyes were so puffy from crying, it hurt to blink.

"Are you okay?" he asked.

"Yeah."

"You don't look okay."

"I'm feeling pretty lousy, actually."

"Laura, will you give me another chance?"

It hurt to move my head or look from side to side. I turned slowly toward him, willing myself not to burst into tears.

"I don't know where it went wrong between us," he said, "but I want to try again. Can we do that?"

I couldn't bear the thought of starting over with Ryan.

"We'll go slow," he said. "You don't have to commit to anything. What about a picnic lunch on a park bench today? We'll do take-out from that deli you like, that awful place with the soggy pickles."

Ryan had a way of tickling my funny bone. And so I said yes to a deli lunch with soggy pickles.

Even in her grief, a girl has to eat.

It was baby steps at first. But Ryan and I slowly recovered, mostly because of his heroic patience.

A week after Gavin told me of Isabelle's pregnancy, he returned to London. We had a last round of Scotch at his favorite jazz bar. I wished him well, but made it clear I wasn't going to be the woman he slept with when he was in New York.

About a month later, I was sipping coffee at my kitchen table on a Sunday morning, reading the *Times*, when a dagger pierced my heart. I was looking at a photo of Gavin and his new bride, Isabelle.

I started to cry, just as Ryan came out of the bathroom after a shower. He had a towel wrapped around his waist, his hair still wet.

"Laura, what's wrong?"

Ryan glanced at Gavin's wedding photo and the caption beneath it. "I can't deny I'm relieved," he said.

He let me cry, as he held me close.

"I'm not asking you to forget him," he said, kissing my hair. "But I hope someday you'll see how right *we* are."

Six months later, Ryan and I were engaged.

With a ring on my finger, I was at an event at MoMA, on assignment, when I saw Gavin across the room. There was no hiding behind a potted plant. He had seen me, too.

I was so stunned, it took me a few minutes to believe I wasn't hallucinating as he made his way toward me.

"You're looking well," he said.

"You, too."

"What do you say we step outside?"

He quickly led me out of the museum and hailed a cab. He asked the driver to take us to our jazz bar.

As we zigzagged through traffic, Gavin reached over and held my hand. The language of hands can be extremely erotic. But the spell of the moment was broken when he fingered my engagement ring.

I was in the thrall of déjà vu as we sat at the bar. Gavin ordered Scotch. I remembered our first night here, knowing I would let him take me to his bed.

"Shall we toast that sparkler on your finger?" he asked as he lifted his glass.

I noticed he wasn't wearing a wedding ring. "Are you one of those guys who doesn't advertise he's married?"

"For good reason."

"Okay, so let's keep it simple – to good art and happy memories." I clinked my glass against his.

After an awkward pause, I recklessly cut to the quick. "Boy or girl?"

"There is no baby. Isabelle miscarried soon after the wedding."

I felt like such a bitch. "I'm sorry, Gavin."

"No need." He took another swig of his Scotch. "Actually, I'm not sure she was ever pregnant."

"Why do you say that?"

"She found out about you."

"How?"

"You and I were seen about town. A friend of hers was at the gallery opening I took you to."

"But how do you fake a pregnancy test?"

Gavin shrugged. "A gynecologist friend of mine says it's easy to do. You just pry open the stick and alter the strip."

"Gavin..."

"Enough about me. Tell me your news," he said, faking a smile. "Have you set a date yet?"

I couldn't say anything for a minute. I let the Scotch coat my tongue, hoping it would give me the words.

He glanced at my ring. "You're really going to do this?" he asked.

"Why shouldn't I?"

"Because you love me?"

"I did."

"Past tense?"

I looked at him defiantly. "You left – and married someone else, and didn't seem to care that I loved you."

"Laura, I thought she was *pregnant*."

During the last few months before my wedding, it wasn't easy putting Gavin from my mind. He was in New York a lot, working as a consultant at MoMA.

We met occasionally at our jazz bar. I had twinges of guilt, feeling like I was cheating on Ryan by just having a drink with Gavin.

There was so much still simmering between Gavin and me. I was dangerously close to succumbing to him. I wanted him and he knew that.

One night at the bar, he leaned over and kissed me.

"Are you happy?" he asked me.

"As happy as I can be, given the trauma of the past six months." His hand was on my thigh. "What about you?" I asked. "What are you going to do?"

At that point, Gavin was spending more time in New York than he was in London with Isabelle.

"I'm done," he said. "It's up to her to file for divorce."

"It seems to me she's got you where she wants you."

"She won't stay in this. I'll give her a year."

"Then what?"

"I'll end it."

One Friday night, well after midnight, my phone rang. It was Gavin. I could tell he was drunk.

"Laura, I love you," he said, slurring his words.

Ryan was in bed next to me and took the phone. "Gavin?" he said. "Leave us the fuck alone."

Ryan calmly hung up and turned to me in the darkness. "If you have any doubts, Laura, tell me now. I don't want that guy in bed with us ever again."

I married Ryan in my hometown in the Chicago suburbs, at the church where I had so many happy memories growing up. Pastor

B officiated. Funny that the minister knew more about my early love life than anyone else at my wedding.

It was a beautiful day. Friends from far and near helped us celebrate. My sister, who was my maid of honor, turned to me as she was about to walk down the aisle. Catching a glimpse of Ryan, she said, "I've never seen a happier groom."

Ryan was beaming as I walked toward him, in measured steps to Beethoven's "Ode to Joy," holding tight to my father's arm. I had no second thoughts that day. I felt sure that everything about this marriage was meant to be, despite my hairpin turn-in-the-road with Gavin.

Of course, my mom and dad were delighted with the choice I had made. My mother never asked about Gavin. She plunged into her role as mother-of-the-bride, happily taking charge of all the arrangements. She couldn't imagine a better son-in-law.

But my father felt a need to put to rest old business. One evening when I was home, about a month before the wedding, he and I had some time alone together. We were sitting on the back porch, crickets chirping, when out of nowhere he asked, "How did you leave things with that guy from London?"

"Gavin is married now."

"Did you see that coming?"

"Yes and no."

"Are you sure about marrying Ryan?"

"Yes."

"A year ago, if you could have chosen between Ryan and Gavin, it seems you would have chosen Gavin."

I nodded. "You're right. I would have."

"So what changed?"

I listened to the crickets for a moment. "Sometimes things happen that change our options."

When my father walked me down the aisle on my wedding day, he knew I had come to this choice partly because the man I loved more than Ryan had married someone else. When Dad gave me away, he kissed my hand. I knew I had his blessing and his hope that I'd know the lasting love he had enjoyed with my mother. I hoped for that, too, with all my heart.

A few months after we married, Ryan and I moved to Los Angeles. He had gotten a big promotion with his firm. I got a job in the press office at the Norton Simon Museum in Pasadena, where Ryan and I bought a little bungalow. The house needed some work, and fixing it up became our favorite pastime. We joined an old-house preservation group and met local artisans who were helping restore Pasadena's many Craftsman-era homes that give the city its architectural charm.

I loved that house and told Ryan, after one exhausting day of sanding woodwork, that I intended to die in that house.

"Me, too," he said. "They can carry us out together."

I can honestly say we were very happily married then. We loved our new life in La La Land – especially the weather and the laid-back southern-California lifestyle. We often spent Sundays at the beach, sometimes not quite believing our good luck – especially on warm winter days when the East Coast was buried in snow.

We liked our jobs and had an active social life with other couples our age who lived in the neighborhood.

I was 35 when I got pregnant with Kyle. Ryan was ecstatic. He went to parenting classes with me and read all the popular childcare books. He loved reading bedtime stories to our babe-in-utero. "I want him to hear my voice so he knows me when he's born."

We were more than ready the day Kyle arrived. He was a big, beautiful boy – 9 pounds, at birth – with a full head of hair. I vividly remember the day Kyle and I came home from the hospital. Ryan made him a little nest of blankets on our bed and we lay down beside him, marveling at this little being we had created.

Ryan looked at me with such love. "I've never been happier in my whole life – except for our wedding day...and all the days since."

I smiled. "Good recovery, luv."

I hope someday you'll see how right WE are Ryan had said to me when I wept over Gavin's wedding photo.

Ryan got his wish.

With our baby snuggled between us, I said to him, "I can't imagine a better man to spend my life with and to have a family with."

It was the first time I had ever seen Ryan cry.

A year after Kyle was born, Ryan left the firm and set up his own design studio with another architect he had met in L.A. I had supported his decision, knowing how much he wanted to carve a niche for himself and focus on projects that would showcase his talents and creative vision. He was 38 and ready to embrace his prime.

I also knew how tough the first years of this new venture would be for us as a family. But I wanted Ryan to be happy and was willing to do whatever I could to help him. I liked his partner, Nate, an outgoing guy with a great sense of humor. He was a good foil to Ryan, who gladly let Nate handle the front-office side of the business.

Their first big break came when they won a design competition for a repertory theater complex to be built near Newport Beach, California. The project started out well, but ran into trouble about six months in. The cash prize from the competition was enough to keep them going initially, but when the owner came up short during the pre-construction phase, Ryan and Nate had to scramble for other work.

I could see the stress taking its toll on Ryan. He wasn't sleeping well. I'd often find him up late at night working on drawings or sometimes he'd be asleep on the living room sofa with a couple of empty beer cans on the coffee table.

Ryan's undoing had a lot to do with his biology.

I had never met Ryan's father, who had died of cancer when Ryan was a teenager. Ryan didn't speak of him much, but I had seen a photo of him – the handsome Irish-American GI with his beautiful Italian war bride on their wedding day in Trieste. In the photo, he's straddling a big motorbike and Lily is in the sidecar, with a corsage pinned to her jacket. They were a gorgeous couple, and according to Ryan, the life of every party.

What Ryan had never told me, until we ended up in marriage counseling, was that his father had been an alcoholic. I was shocked that he had kept this from me. Ryan didn't seem to think it was something he needed to discuss. He was in total denial about the impact his father's addiction had had on him. But during our therapy sessions, it became evident how much trauma and heartache Ryan had suppressed.

We ended up in therapy after a July 4th family picnic with friends. Ryan had gotten drunk during the course of the afternoon and evening. At first, he was downing cans of beer like they were sodas. Then I saw him hitting the Jim Beam. When it came time to leave after the fireworks, I asked him to give me the car keys and he refused. With an audience of our closest friends watching, he became belligerent, berating me for thinking that he couldn't drive home.

Nate intervened and pried the keys from him. As Nate turned to me, Ryan took a wild swing at him. He missed, but the punch, if it had landed, would have knocked Nate off his feet.

Ryan lunged at him. "Gimme those keys, you son of a bitch."

Nate grabbed him by the shoulders and pinned him against a lamppost. "What the fuck is wrong with you?"

Two other guys stepped in and kept Nate from throwing a punch of his own.

The worst part of it was that Kyle, then 3, stood next to me, clinging to my skirt and sobbing.

After several counseling sessions, our therapist urged Ryan to start rehab. Ryan and I hardly spoke on the way home that evening, with me at the wheel. I wondered if we'd ever recover from this.

I drove the babysitter home that night. When I got back a half hour later, I found Ryan sitting at the side of our bed, in the dark.

I sat down next to him and held his hand.

What he said next tore a hole in me.

"You would have been so much happier if you had married Gavin," he said.

Ryan didn't know that Gavin hadn't stopped contacting me. Whenever he was in L.A., Gavin would call and invite me to lunch. I always said no. But there was a part of me that wanted to say yes. As my marriage unraveled, I often thought about seeing Gavin again. Sometimes when Ryan and I went through the motions of making love, I fantasized about Gavin, remembering how he could make me feel.

But that night, on the edge of our bed, I looked at Ryan, in the depths of his despair. I had chosen Ryan, for better or worse, in sickness and in health. Ryan was sick. I wanted him to get better. I still wanted to have a life with him and raise a son with him.

I leaned over and kissed his cheek. "I want *you*."

Ryan spent a month in rehab. He and Nate tried to regroup after their devastating rupture at the July 4th picnic. But they decided in the end to close the design studio. Ryan took a job at a small architectural firm in Pasadena. We had a steady income again, which was good.

But Ryan was angry at the world. At times, that anger was directed at me. He'd flare at me for the littlest things. Sometimes he'd turn on Kyle, which I wouldn't tolerate.

One Saturday, the three of us were at the beach. Ryan was enjoying a good book, so I offered to go back to the car to put money in the parking meter.

"I think we should move our things back a bit," I said to Ryan. "The tide is coming in."

The tongue of a wave suddenly spilled over the wall of a castle Kyle was building.

"Oh, no!" Kyle cried. "Daddy, will you help me save my castle?"

Ryan, engrossed in his book, didn't respond.

"Ryan?"

He looked up at me. "What?"

"The meter is going to expire in 10 minutes and a castle needs saving."

"Go. I got this."

I was gone about 25 minutes. When I came back, there were paramedics on the beach. The child they had rescued was Kyle.

Kyle was wild-eyed and wailing, in the arms of a paramedic, when he saw me running toward him. I'll never forget the terror on his face. "Mommy! Mommy!" he screamed.

I scooped him in my arms and held him tight. "Sweetie, I'm here."

Ryan was talking to a policeman. I turned to a lifeguard. "What happened?"

"I saw it all from the chair," he said. "Your husband went into the water and the boy followed. Poor little guy got tumbled pretty hard by a wave."

I looked at Ryan in disbelief. He had waded into the surf to cool off, leaving his four-year-old son alone on the beach.

As the crowd dispersed and the paramedics packed up their gear, I watched my husband talk his way out of an arrest for child endangerment. But the officer lit into him, reprimanding him for his negligence.

I turned away from Ryan, cradling our son in my arms.

"Mommy, I couldn't breathe," Kyle said, hiccups punctuating his words.

Rubbing his back, I kissed his damp curls. "Sweetie, I'm so sorry."

I looked out at the sea, the surface twinkling with sparkles of light. It should have been a lovely day at the beach.

I heard Ryan folding up the chairs and throwing Kyle's sand toys into the bucket. I didn't move. I couldn't look at him.

Eventually, he called out to me. "Shall we go?"

Still holding Kyle, I walked some distance behind Ryan. My heart was pounding, my head throbbing.

When we got to the car, I put Kyle in his car seat. He fell sleep before we even got to the freeway.

Only then did I look at Ryan. "What were you thinking?"

"Don't start with me. I told him to stay on the blanket."

"He's four years old..."

"I said don't start with me!"

We rode in silence for the next hour. It was then that I made up my mind.

The next day, I called a divorce attorney.

I remember how tenderly Ryan kissed me on our wedding day. "I love you so much, Laura," he whispered. "I'll never let you down." He had fought so hard to win me back after I had strayed with Gavin. I didn't think for a second that he wouldn't love and cherish me till the end of our days.

When Kyle was born, I couldn't imagine how we could be happier. I was so in love with Ryan then, the new father who wept with joy as he cuddled his infant son.

Why do we throw away happiness? Why do we tempt fate to take away everything we love?

We can blame our demons. I blame Ryan's. But I often wonder if I did enough to help him fight them. At what point do you cut your losses and get out, knowing you did all you could?

I try not to shoulder blame for not rescuing him. There are times when we have to accept that some outcomes are beyond our control.

~4~

The Tenor of Venice

"Lady, are you lost?" he asked.

I was looking at a map of Venice, with my roller bag at my side.

"Yes, I'm a little lost," I admitted to a dark-eyed, swarthy stranger in a tight T-shirt, who was craning his neck to see my map. I had never seen such colorfully tattooed biceps in my life. I usually appreciate the kindness of strangers, but this guy wasn't someone I would have approached for directions. Nonetheless, I showed him where I had marked my hotel with an asterisk on the map.

He pointed to the narrow walkway where I had spent the last 10 minutes looking for No. 1008. But he had never heard of the hotel.

I was grateful he didn't offer to accompany me on my search. I found a payphone nearby and called the number for the hotel, listed in my guidebook. This was 1995 – most tourists weren't traveling with cell phones yet. The woman who answered didn't speak English. It was hopeless getting directions from her. Turns out, she was a maid who had been passing by the reception desk when the phone rang.

I was literally 10 steps from the front door, which had no sign, no number.

Ah, Venice. Lost at hello.

It was a fitting beginning to this trip. I was just divorced. Kyle was with Ryan at Grandma Lily's annual family gathering on Maryland's Eastern Shore. I had two weeks to call my own. I wanted to wander off and get lost somewhere. Venice seemed like the perfect place.

I had visited Venice during my spring-break trip in 1975, when I traveled with a group of Oxford friends to Italy. Our first stop was Venice.

My memory of that weeklong visit is shrouded in drizzly gloom. It rained constantly, with rising water from the lagoon soaking our shoes and the hems of our jeans. After I peeled off my wet clothes one night, I tested my immune system at the sink in my tiny room at the pensione where we stayed. I drank three glasses of tap water before I went to bed that night. If I was going to get sick from microbes I had ingested, I wanted to get over it as soon as possible. Miraculously, the next morning I was fine. The cheap local wine we were consuming in copious amounts may have been the perfect antidote.

But here I was, 20 years later, on my own, in the bright light of a splendid summer's day in Venice. Unfortunately, my jet lag was overtaking me. I had been traveling for 30-some hours and my odyssey by bus and boat from the Venice airport had taken the last bit of oomph out of me. I badly needed a bed and room service.

I rang the doorbell at what I hoped was No. 1008. The push button on the brass panel was shiny from use – a clue that this might be a frequently visited location on what seemed to be a quiet canal in the backwater of Venice.

Enrico, the hotel manager, appeared. He greeted me warmly and, with my bag in hand, escorted me upstairs. He made quick work of checking me in, sensing I was on my last legs. When he opened the door to my room, I felt like I was time traveling. The walls were covered in golden brocade and adorned with amber Murano-glass sconces. The old wooden bed had a canopy draped in vintage lace. On the mantel of the fireplace, opposite the bed, was an antique clock stuck at 6:30, along with two porcelain figures – a woman singing from a songbook and a man who appeared to be a courtly Casanova type. Although the room was newly refurbished, Enrico told me the dark, timbered ceiling was 1,200 years old.

My watch said 3:30 a.m. California time. Half past noon in Venice, my resting spot for the next week. After Enrico disappeared, I closed the shutters and undressed. I slipped under the covers and fell asleep to the song of a tenor whose beautiful voice floated outside my window.

I felt a bit wobbly on my first night in Venice. I didn't wander far from the hotel for dinner. Enrico had recommended a trattoria close by. I glanced at the posted menu before the maître d' approached. He wore a tux that he filled out nicely and a nametag that read Antonio. He had thick, graying hair and a devilish sparkle in his eyes.

"*Signora.*" He bowed slightly. "*Sola?*"

"Yes, I'm alone."

He winked at me. "You won't feel lonely here."

Antonio seated me at a table by the canal, the same canal I looked down on from my hotel window. A gondola passed by. I gazed with envy at the passengers – a young couple who were enjoying what I hoped, for them, would be a romantic night they'd never forget.

I studied the menu. Lobster salad with fried zucchini blossoms caught my eye.

A waiter brought a complimentary *antipasto* appetizer and a glass of prosecco. Ten minutes later, Antonio re-appeared.

"What would please you?" he asked in English.

"The lobster salad."

"We don't have," he said brusquely.

"Ohhhh," I said with disappointment.

He shrugged. "They don't deliver fish on Monday."

"What fish do you have?"

"We have scallops," he said, pointing to the scallop-and-mushroom risotto on the list of the day's specials.

"Do you recommend it?"

"*È delizioso, signora.*"

I ordered the risotto, which was delicious, just as Antonio had promised. He tried to tempt me with a second course, but I declined.

"*Un dolce?*" he asked, showing me the dessert menu.

I suddenly felt queasy. My stomach had no idea what time zone we were in. "*No, grazie,*" I replied. "Maybe tomorrow."

He smiled. "*A domani.*"

A few minutes later, he served me a shot of *limoncello*. "You will sleep well tonight."

I did sleep well. So well, in fact, that I was jolted awake the next morning by a knock at my door. For a moment, I wasn't sure where I was as I looked up at the lacy bed canopy. I threw on my robe and cracked open the door, relieved to see a lovely young woman holding my breakfast tray, laden with pastries, and importantly, a pot of coffee.

As she set the tray on a table by the window, I opened the shutters to greet the day. It was still early. The walkway by the canal was deserted except for a baker, in his white apron, tossing breadcrumbs to a flock of cooing pigeons.

The morning sunlight crept along the surface of the canal, where the rippled reflection of the buildings created a wavy, bargello effect in a palette of sea green, mustardy ochre and burnt umber.

A small motorboat, carrying a load of produce, obliterated the watery painting under the foam of its wake. I was mesmerized watching the reflections reconfigure themselves.

I understood why painters come to Venice, in hopes of capturing the visual magic that happens here. The shape-shifting reflections and vapory light play tricks on the eyes. Fractured sunbeams dance on the underside of a bridge. The diaphanous fog and mist seem almost touchable, like the cobwebby recesses of the mind during sleep.

I poured coffee and devoured a flaky brioche that likely was the artistry of the baker who fed the pigeons. No wonder they gathered at his feet. I couldn't stop at one. The second was even better.

After a steamy hot shower, I stepped naked into the room just as I heard the tenor. It was the same incredible voice from the day before. I threw on my robe and hurried to the window.

With wet hair and a costume made of terry cloth, I was hardly presentable to this man with the extraordinary voice. I hadn't expected him to notice me, standing at a window two stories above him. But it was a moment of serendipitous circumstances.

To my surprise, this little backwater canal suddenly had become clogged with gondolas. I soon realized the problem. There was a low-clearance bridge at the next *calle* – as the narrow streets in Venice are called. One particularly tall gondolier was nearly bent double as he cautiously navigated his boat full of tourists under the low arch of the bridge.

The waiting gondolas in the queue were gridlocked. The tenor had a captive audience.

He was a robustly handsome man with a grand operatic voice that reverberated off the ancient brick-and-stone palazzos that lined the canal. I noticed others were peering from their windows, too. We had balcony seats to an incredible performance.

The tenor sang "Nessun Dorma" – made famous by Luciano Pavarotti – from Giacomo Puccini's opera *Turandot*.

I grew up listening to this magnificent aria. My father was an opera buff and had a recording of *Turandot* that he played often.

I loved the story, which is set in China. Calaf, a man of mystery who's really a prince, falls in love – god knows why – with steel-hearted, sociopathic Princess Turandot, who has a nasty habit of beheading her suitors if they can't answer her three riddles. When Calaf answers them correctly, she freaks out and refuses to marry him. Then Calaf makes her an offer: If she can guess his name before dawn of the next day, she can kill him. If not, she must marry him. The princess proclaims that none of her subjects will be allowed to sleep that night until someone discovers his name. Failing that, everyone will die. Frankly, I'm really not sure what Calaf saw in her.

At the opening of the final act, he's alone in the palace's moonlit garden, hearing the command of the royal heralds in the distance: *Nessun dorma! No one sleeps!*

Calaf is pretty damn sure of himself as he sings...

> *No one sleeps! No one sleeps!*
> *Not even you, oh Princess*
> *in your cold bedroom,*
> *watching the stars*
> *that tremble with love and with hope!*

> *...Vanish, o night!*
> *Fade, you stars!*
> *Fade, you stars!*
> *At dawn, I will win!*
> *I will win! I will win!*

Of course, this aria must be sung in its original Italian. Calaf's shouts of triumph at the end – *Vincerò! Vincerò! Vincerò!* – move audiences to cheers and tears.

That last verse always feels like a sexual climax to me. No matter who the tenor, I let him sweep me away.

I had never seen this aria performed in an intimate venue, where I could see the fire of passion in the tenor's eyes. But on that day, from my perch above the canal, the Tenor sang to me...

> *Ma il mio mistero è chiuso in me;*
> *il nome mio nessun saprà!*
> *No, no! Sulla tua bocca*
> *Io dirò quando la luce splenderà!*
> *Ed il mio bacio scioglierà*
> *il silenzio che ti fa mia!*

Although my Italian was spotty, I knew the English translation by heart: But my secret is hidden within me. No one will know my name. On your mouth I will say it when the light shines...and my kiss will dissolve the silence that makes you mine.

The Tenor stood, looking up at me, with one foot braced on the gondola's bow, as he belted out...

> *Vincerò! Vincerò! Vincerò!*

The crowd that had gathered on the walkway by the canal roared with approval as the Tenor held his heart-stopping high note with his hand to his chest.

It was an amazing scene. The gondolier maneuvered to the side of the canal as the cheering crowd pushed forward, tossing money into the front of the gondola. A young boy, who had been sitting at the bow, scooped it up, allowing the Tenor to enjoy his moment. The Tenor bowed and then looked up at me and waved.

The gondolas began moving. I impulsively took the red rose from the bud vase on my breakfast tray and tossed it to him. He nearly lost his balance as he reached up to catch it. He reminded me of me, adeptly fielding bridal bouquets.

"Bravo!" I shouted, blowing him a kiss.

Grinning, he blew one back to me.

I strolled around Venice that day with a spring in my step.

Still swooning from that performance on the canal, I felt drawn to Venice's famous opera house La Fenice, which was a short walk from the hotel. I was happy to discover it was open and bought a ticket for a self-guided audio tour.

On that day, in 1995, I saw La Fenice in its authentic 19th-century glory. At that time, it had been rebuilt twice after devastating fires – in 1774 and 1836 – earning its name, which translates as "The Phoenix" in English. The next year, in 1996, the opera house would be destroyed again by fire, at the hands of two electricians who torched the place to dodge hefty fines because they were behind on their contract to do repairs. The company's owner fled and, after his capture at the border of Mexico and Belize, was extradited back to Italy to serve his prison term. A modern-day opera plot in its own right.

When La Fenice re-opened in 2003, the new design closely copied the theater's former 19th-century style, with tiers of elegantly decorated box seats rimming the majestic horseshoe-shaped hall. But I'll never forget seeing La Fenice as it was, from the era of Giuseppe Verdi, who premiered his operas *Ernani, Attila, Rigoletto, La Traviata* and *Simon Boccanegra* there in the mid-1800s.

My audio tour that day led me from the opera house's opulent ballroom to a corridor with numbered doors that accessed the first tier of box seats. To my delight, there was a rehearsal in progress for Verdi's *Otello*. My tour included a stop at the Royal Box, so I eagerly took a seat.

When I was a teenager, my father used to take me to performances at the Chicago Lyric Opera. I was 14 when I saw *Otello* for the first time, with world-famous Canadian heldentenor Jon Vickers in the title role as the exotic Moor. I was mesmerized by Vickers, who commanded a massive presence on stage. His eyes, set off by blackface makeup, burned with emotion in his fits of lust and rage. The powerful timbre of his voice nearly pinned me to the back of my seat. I was breathless by the end of that performance.

The Fenice singers playing Otello and his wife, Desdemona, were rehearsing their love duet at the end of Act 1. Otello has just returned from a naval battle and they're wildly happy to see each other.

The set was a contemporary design, featuring a huge rotating box with a missing side that revealed a bedroom. The soprano playing Desdemona leaned back on the bed as Otello knelt on the floor beside her, removing one of her shoes. His hands fumbled under the folds of her long, billowing, black skirt, making it appear he was going for more than her other shoe. But then he got up and stepped out of the box, as it swiveled, onto a terrace and started singing to a golden angel floating above the stage.

The young Italian director took charge, clearly wanting to heighten the sexual tension. First, he had Desdemona coquettishly woo Otello back to the bedroom. On the next run-through, he decided Otello should tenderly hold her in his arms as they gazed at the stars and then, in a surge of passion, pin her to the terrace wall as he's about to kiss her. In a nice twist, the director ended the scene with Desdemona pushing away Otello's arm and taking his hand – leading him to bed.

The director wanted to see the scene from the top, which meant rotating the bedroom box back to its original position. The stagehands in charge of spinning the box missed their cue, which prompted the director to stop the scene and impatiently yell, "Yoo-hoo!"

The giggle from the Royal Box was mine.

At the end of the tour, I lingered at the gift shop and bought a book about La Fenice for my father, along with some postcards. Phones with cameras and photo-sharing apps hadn't been invented yet. I loved the travel ritual of writing postcards. I tucked my Fenice cards inside my journal, intending to find a café table to use as my desk.

I checked my map to get my bearings, then threw myself into the maze of Venice.

It was early June. The summer bustle had begun. Delivery men and hotel porters, pushing trolleys stacked with boxes and luggage, tangled with tourists on the winding, narrow streets.

I was following signs pointing the way to Piazza San Marco. The signage in Venice requires a leap of faith, especially when an arrow takes a crooked turn. My map wasn't much help, so I hoped for the best.

In a moment of confusion, I had wandered down a side street where a shop window caught my eye. Gorgeous hand-knitted garments were on display alongside baskets of beautiful yarn. Italy is known for its knitting wool. My mother, an expert knitter, paid a premium for Italian yarn and made lovely sweaters, scarves and hats for my sister and me of cashmere, angora, mohair and Merino wool.

I never excelled as a knitter. My mom taught me how to knit when I was about 8. But I couldn't master the skill of picking up dropped stitches – and invariably, I seemed to have a lot of them. I'd watch her patiently weave the lost loop up through the rows, from where I'd left the stitch behind. To me, it was like witnessing a magic act.

I suddenly felt inspired to knit again, seeing the window of the yarn shop. I went inside and spent the next hour with a lovely Italian woman, about my age, and her mother, admiring their artful creations. I chose yarn for a simple scarf that wouldn't require too much technical ability and a few skeins of fine cashmere for my mom. I bought a set of bamboo needles for my project, which I was eager to begin.

Later that afternoon, I stopped by the trattoria where I'd had dinner the night before. Antonio greeted me with an air kiss on each cheek.

"Is it too early for a cocktail?" I asked him.

He smiled. "*Signora*, it is Italy. It is never too early."

He seated me at table along the canal. I ordered a glass of prosecco and watched a gondola approach. An accordion player on board played *O Sole Mio*, which made my heart ache a little.

I opened my bag from the yarn shop and took out the needles and a skein of the yarn I had chosen for my scarf. The yarn was imbued with the colors of Venice on that summery day – bright cobalt blue, mossy green and lemon yellow. Tiny sequins that mimicked the pinpoints of sunlight on the surface of the canal were woven into the fibers.

I cast on 20 stitches and was on my third row when Antonio returned with my prosecco and a tray of nibbles.

"Are you making that for me?" he asked.

I nodded. "I think the sequins will look good on you."

"I think they will look beautiful on you," he said, admiring my work-in-progress. The yarn was spun with loopy clusters that formed florets as you knit. "Will you be coming here tonight for dinner?"

"Do you have lobster today?"

He shook his head. "Not today."

"You said that yesterday."

"Come tonight and I will have the chef make you something wonderful."

It was my intention to return for dinner. But when I got back to the hotel, a surprise awaited me.

Enrico was at the front desk when I went to collect my room key. "You have a visitor," he said quietly.

"That's not possible. I don't know anyone in Venice except for two ladies who knit and a maître d'."

Enrico arched an eyebrow. "It seems you've caught the *attenzione* of someone else. He's waiting in the lounge."

"Who is he?"

Enrico smiled. "I cannot say."

Several couples were in the lounge for *aperitivo* hour. I glanced around the room and noticed a man sitting at the bar, alone, talking to the bartender. I couldn't see his face at first. But as if sensing my presence, he turned toward me.

It was the Tenor.

He quickly stood and made his way across the room.

I was so stunned I couldn't move.

"*Signorina...*" He stopped short when he saw the shock on my face. "I've surprised you. I hope not in a bad way."

"No. I mean yes." I felt myself wilting a little. "I'm very surprised. But it's a nice surprise."

"Good." He took a deep breath. I sensed he was a little nervous, too. "I'm so happy to see you." He motioned to a table in the corner. "Will you join me for a drink?"

I hesitated for an instant.

"Please say yes."

I was riveted to his dark, soulful eyes. "How can I say no to the man who sang to me this morning?"

In that moment, I knew my holiday in Venice wasn't going to be spent knitting a scarf.

The tenor's name was Stefano.

The spell Stefano had cast over me that morning as he sang from the gondola continued at the hotel bar that evening. He was charming and fascinating, full of stories of growing up in Venice. His mother had worked as a costumer at La Fenice. His father was a violin maker.

Music was in Stefano's veins. He had attended a local music academy as a teenager and decided to apprentice with his father.

"But I learned I didn't have the patience to make violins," he told me. "So I got a degree in marketing and now help my father with his business."

"You have such a beautiful voice," I said to him. "Have you thought of performing?"

He smiled. "You mean aside from singing on gondolas?"

I hoped I hadn't offended him. "Yes. You should be on the stage."

"*Grazie.*" He took a sip of his Negroni. "My cousin owns the gondola. I'm good for business. I enjoy singing for the tourists, actually. I give them a good memory of Venice."

Stefano wanted to know my story. "Is this your first time in Venice?"

"I was here as a student, 20 years ago, for a short visit."

"You're traveling alone?"

"Yes."

He glanced at my left hand. "You're not married?"

"No."

"A beautiful woman like you?"

"I'm recently divorced."

"I'm sorry. I shouldn't ask such questions."

I fingered the stem of my wine glass, wondering if he was married.

"How long will you stay?" he asked.

"A week."

"And then?"

"I'll go to Florence and Rome."

Stefano reached across the table and took my hand. "May I see you again?"

His question hung in the air for a moment as I contemplated what was about to happen.

"My uncle has a restaurant. We could have dinner there. His seafood dishes are the best in Venice."

He squeezed my hand. "Say yes. *Per favore.*"

I smiled at him.

"I'll pick you up tomorrow at 8."

I woke up early the next morning, to the sound of the baker's cooing pigeons feasting on their breakfast.

From somewhere in the distance, a gondolier shouted "*Oy-ee!*" – the call of caution on the canals.

I opened the shutters to discover a thick mist had rolled in overnight.

My breakfast tray wouldn't be arriving for another hour. I threw on jeans and a sweater and headed out to watch Venice wake up.

The cry of a baby pierced the stillness as I walked down a narrow *calle* that snaked between peeling stucco facades. A set of weathered wooden shutters the color of seaweed creaked open on their rusty hinges above me. I caught a glimpse of an old man peering down at me, *la straniera* – the foreigner – who was intruding on the last moments of solitude before the day began.

A buxom young woman leaned from a third-floor window, pegging a pair of jeans to the clothesline strung across the *calle* to the apartment window opposite hers. I stifled a giggle when she hung an enormous red satin bra on the line. The squeal of the pulley as she let her C cups unfurl no doubt echoed the delight of her neighborhood admirers.

Approaching Piazza San Marco, I found myself at the Orseolo Basin, a popular gondola station that serves as a gondola parking area by night. At that early hour, the basin was quiet, except for the sound of a couple dozen moored gondolas – perfectly aligned side-by-side in short rows – gently nudging each other, water slapping the hulls.

From around the corner at the far end of the basin, a gondola appeared with a slender, tall boy in his late teens at the helm. An older man, wearing a red-and-white striped gondolier's jersey, stood behind his young protégé, with a firm hand on the end of the oar as together they steered the gondola to a loading dock near the footbridge where I stood bearing witness to an ancient Venetian tradition pass from one generation to the next.

It was when they drew close to the dock that I saw the resemblance. The boy was so strikingly like him, it took my breath away.

In a whisper, I said his name for the first time in 20 years. *Luca.*

Luca and I met in Venice when I was 20 and he was 19. He worked in the pizzeria below the *pensione* where my Oxford friends and I stayed on our spring-break trip.

Luca's family owned the pizzeria. The entire staff was family – uncles, aunts, siblings, cousins. Luca's mother worked the register and his dad worked the bar. Luca – an acrobatic pizza-dough tosser – was the entertainment.

Luca had a talent that would have made him a viral sensation if YouTube had been around then. He could toss and twirl orbs of thin, stretched pizza dough like they were giant frisbees. He'd send them spinning toward the ceiling and catch them on a fingertip. Then with a toss behind his back, they'd roll across his shoulder blades and down one arm. His signature move was throwing a whirling dough disc between his legs while doing an aerial split. This required some room. The patrons happily moved the tables to clear some floor space.

Our jolly group had dinner every night at the pizzeria and Luca quickly became one of us. He joined us on our roamings around Venice. We had a fabulous time with him as our guide.

Luca's parents owned the *pensione* and his mother doted on us like we were her own children. She fussed about drying our rain-soaked clothes and would bring a basket to the breakfast room each morning with our jeans slightly toasty from a space heater that had served as a dryer.

On our first night, Luca's mother appeared at my door holding several small flannel sacks with drawstrings. She saw my bewildered expression and opened a compartment above the radiator where thin terra-cotta bricks were waiting to heat my bed. She slipped the bricks into the sacks and tucked them under the bed covers. I had become accustomed to curling up at night with a hot water bottle in my chilly dorm room at Oxford. But that night in Venice, as rain pelted my window, I dreamt I was lying on a warm sandy beach.

When we checked into the *pensione*, I gladly took the tiny single room on the top floor. The other two girls in our group of six stayed in a double room on the middle floor and the guys camped out on the sofas in the reception area downstairs. Up to that point in our travels, we had been sleeping in train compartments using each other as pillows. At Luca's place, we felt like we had bagged a five-star hotel.

We paid next to nothing for our lodging and were happy to help out at the pizzeria to earn our keep. With my waitressing experience, I had a little-known skillset that amused my British travel mates, who had never worked a day in their lives. But I could tell Luca was impressed.

I soon graduated from table-setter to pizza maker. I must confess that was a bit of a leap, considering I nearly failed cooking in my junior-high Home Ec class. But with Luca as my mentor, I was eager to accept the challenge.

I had a crush on Luca. From the moment he offered to carry my heavy backpack to my attic bedroom, I knew that my heart had a soft spot for Italian men. I would struggle with this predilection in years to come. But at the age of 20, I was more than willing to succumb to it.

Luca and I were shaping dough one afternoon at a long marble-top table in the pizzeria kitchen when I knew he looked at me as more than his apprentice.

I was all thumbs as I tried to flatten the dough ball.

"*Cosi*, like this," he said, turning my right hand on its side.

He held my hand in his as we pressed against the rim of the thick dough round to make a raised outer edge.

"With this one," he said, gently guiding my left hand, "we move the dough in a circle."

We soon had a rhythm, his arms around me as we pushed and stretched the dough.

"You're very good at this," he said.

Luca had learned English from tourist customers, many of them students, who, like my group, couldn't afford upscale restaurants. He had an ear for American slang and had a good command of colorful verbs when it came to describing the culinary art of pizza making.

Dusting the table with more flour, he smiled at me. "Now I teach you to slap it."

I tried not to laugh. But my mind had wandered to someplace below the table.

"What is so funny?" he asked.

His cheek brushed against mine. I badly wanted him to kiss me. I know he knew that. But I still had a lot to learn about the Italian male.

That night, I didn't have a chance to show off my dough-slapping prowess. Luca's cousin Rosa, the head waitress, called in sick. I put on an apron and instantly was in my element. I didn't realize at the outset that not only was Rosa the head waitress, she was the only waitress scheduled to work that night.

It took me a few orders to master the vocabulary of Italian pizza toppings. *Peperoni*, in Italian, is peppers, not salami. *Salamino* is salami. *Salsiccia* is sausage. *Würstel* is basically chopped-up frankfurters. *Speck* is cured, smoked pork similar to bacon that's popular in northern Italy, not to be confused with *prosciutto*, which is cured ham often served raw. The cheese offerings were mozzarella and creamy *stracchino*, made from the milk of cows that graze in Alpine meadows. The beverage menu was easy: a red house wine, a local beer and Coca-Cola.

I made a map of the room on the back of my order pad and numbered the tables. I was a model of efficiency and smiling American customer service. The patrons were wowed, especially my Oxford pals. The place was packed and no one wanted to leave. Not just because of the hospitality. It rained like crazy that night. Luca's Uncle Guido piled sandbags at the door to keep the rising lagoon at bay.

When Luca served me the last pizza from the kitchen that night, he kissed my cheek. "*Per la mia cara.*"

A little while later, after all of the customers had gone, Luca sat down next to me with a jug of wine. The Brits were already half lit.

"We need to catch up with them," I said to Luca as he poured.

Uncle Guido appeared with his accordion and soon we were all dancing. The wine made me feel light on my feet as Luca moved with me to the music.

I fell into my bed in the wee hours, exhausted but happy. I was almost asleep when I heard a faint knock. The door opened slowly.

"Laura…"

Luca quietly closed the door behind him and walked over to the bed. "I will leave if you want me to," he said.

He sat down on the bed next to me. I couldn't see his face in the darkness. He leaned closer and whispered, "I want to spend the night with you."

I didn't need those terra-cotta bed warmers that night. I had Luca.

I love that I lost my virginity to him. I had thought for a long time that Marc would be the one. After all, he gave me my first orgasm that summer's night after a Dairy Queen blizzard.

But surrendering my chastity to a very sexy Italian pizza maestro on a stormy night in Venice is what dreams of gold are all about.

What surprised me most about my fling with Luca was that although I loved every minute of it, I didn't for a moment believe that anything would come of it. For a few days, I slipped into another world, far from the one I knew. I learned to make love and pizza and would never forget or regret any of it.

The phone in my room rang exactly at 8.

It was Enrico. "*Buonasera, signora.* A gentleman is here to see you."

I took a deep breath and one last look in the mirror. This was my first date since my divorce. I was a little nervous, but it helped that I was a few thousand miles from home. I was grateful for the chance to be an anonymous, exotic creature in a distant land.

Stefano was waiting in the lobby. I can still see him in his flaxen linen jacket, with the top buttons of his shirt undone, looking very suave and sexy. He smiled at me as I walked down the stairs, as if to say *you're all mine tonight.*

"How beautiful you are," he said, kissing me on both cheeks.

He waved good night to Enrico, who said something to him in Italian that made Stefano laugh. Enrico winked at me. "I told him to behave himself."

"I'll bring her back before dawn," Stefano said. "Or maybe not."

Enrico pretended to look worried. "*Signora*, you can call me. I'm here all night."

I liked that Enrico was looking out for me.

It was a lovely evening. Stefano offered me his arm as we walked. "I've been looking forward to this all day," he said.

"Me, too."

I couldn't quite believe I wasn't dreaming all this – walking through Venice on the arm of a ridiculously gorgeous Italian guy who had serenaded me from a gondola.

We meandered down quiet walkways away from the crowded tourist routes and crossed a small footbridge, which I remembered from the day before, that led to La Fenice.

"I want to show you something," Stefano said. He took me down a narrow *calle* beside the opera house, along a canal. At the rear of the building was a wooden dock under a glass and wrought-iron canopy.

"Many years ago, this was the grand entrance of La Fenice where nobility would arrive by gondola for a night at the opera.

Can you imagine it?" Stefano said. "The women in their beautiful gowns and jewels..."

"And you, the tenor they all came to hear."

Stefano laughed. "It would have been a great life. There was a famous tenor in Verdi's time whose personal gondola would wait for him here at the dock after his performances. The gondolas were very different then. Much more private. His wife would leave the opera house by the other door, by the piazza. His mistress would wait for him on the gondola."

I could see myself as the mistress in the gondola, waiting for the tenor. I was the modern-day personification of her on that summer's night.

At that moment, I understood the fantasies that feed travel romance. The reality of my normal life back home was slipping away into the magical vapor of Venice.

Stefano put his arm around my waist. "Are you hungry?" he asked.

"Famished."

That night turned into a weather event of Biblical magnitude.

Stefano and I were enjoying drinks at a table outside his Uncle Luigi's trattoria when several waiters appeared with ladders and frantically started unfastening the awning above us.

"*Una brutta tempesta*," one waiter told us, pointing to a black sky behind us.

Stefano jumped to his feet and helped roll up the awning.

I grabbed our wine glasses and headed inside with the other customers.

The indoor seating was upstairs. A group of Germans took charge, pushing the tables together in long rows and rearranging the chairs. I suddenly felt like I was in a Bavarian beer hall.

A lashing rain quickly flooded the narrow *calle* outside the restaurant. Hail the size of mothballs began hitting the windows so hard I thought the glass might crack.

I could hear yelling down below – and laughing. I went partway down the stairs to have a look. The entry had flooded and water was moving toward the kitchen. Stefano, Uncle Luigi, the waiters and two cooks were armed with big push brooms, mops and buckets. They clearly had done this before and seemed to regard it as a team sport. With impressive synchronicity, they swept the torrent of hailstones back into the *calle* and piled sandbags at the door.

Stefano, his shirt wet with rain and sweat, looked up at me and grinned. "Would you like to look at a menu?"

There was no ordering from the menu that night. The cooks went into emergency mode and served up a feast for the stranded. Platters of seafood appeared, along with bowls of steaming pasta. At one point, the power went out, which delayed the next course but added to the ambiance. Uncle Luigi lit candles and poured more wine. The Germans drank like fish.

The storm raged for more than an hour. The *calle* outside the restaurant was white with slush. I looked down at my sandals and dreaded the long walk back to the hotel.

As if reading my mind, Stefano said, "Uncle Luigi might let you borrow his *stivaloni*."

"I'm afraid to ask…"

"Boots for wading. They come up to here." He leaned closer and slid his finger up the side of my leg to my thigh. "You're not exactly dressed for the weather."

"It was a summery June evening a few hours ago."

"I have another idea."

I could tell by the twinkle in his eyes that his idea had nothing to do with taking me back to the hotel that night.

We ended up at his place, which conveniently was just a couple of blocks away. But in the rain, with water around our ankles, it was slow going. My feet were numb, ice chunks between my toes, by the time we got to his front door.

I caught a glimpse of a grand piano in the *salotto*, but we didn't linger there. Stefano led me into the bathroom and turned on the shower. He took a fluffy towel from the cupboard. Shivering, I had started to unbutton my blouse. And then it just happened. Spontaneous combustion under the spray of a hot shower.

We made love most of the night in his big bed. I still remember the silky feel of the sheets, the scent of his cologne that had permeated the pillowcases. I fell asleep shortly before dawn and when I awoke a few hours later, I smelled coffee. Years later, Abbie would tell me, "The wonderful thing about an Italian lover is that he'll make you breakfast the next morning."

I spent the next few days with Stefano.

He was uncomfortable with the idea of staying with me at the hotel, so I slept at his place. I'd show up at the hotel once a day to get clean clothes, and on one of my return visits, Enrico was at the front desk. "You're making easy work for the housekeeping staff," he said, raising an eyebrow.

Stefano laughed when I told him Enrico seemed scandalized. "Enrico is a modern-day Casanova, except he likes men."

"Enrico is gay?"

That made Stefano laugh even harder. "I've known Enrico since we were boys in school together. He was gay even then."

Stefano had a small motorboat that was our mode of transport. I loved seeing the city from the water. Venice is such an improbable place – 117 islands built on a slowly sinking foundation of petrified wood. The sea seems so eager to swallow her whole, but somehow she manages to hang on.

I felt like we were in a Canaletto painting one afternoon as Stefano maneuvered around gondolas on the Grand Canal, nearly swamping one of them. The gondolier started swearing at Stefano and then burst out laughing. It was Stefano's cousin.

"Where have you been?" he shouted.

Stefano shrugged and pointed at me. "I've been busy."

Our destination that day was the island of Burano. Its brightly colored houses line the narrow canals where fishing boats are tethered to timber posts. Intricately woven fishing nets, draped on the posts to dry in the sea breeze, almost look like the creations of the women of Burano who make the island's famous lace.

Stefano bought me a lace handkerchief that day, "*per ricordarti di me*," he said – to remember him by. I fingered the delicate stitches, knowing I'd never forget him.

It was our last day together. He made dinner for me that night at his place and played on his grand piano. And then he took out a violin made by his father and played a nocturne by Borodin.

I should have known then. But that night was a poignant blur, tinged with both joy and sadness.

When Stefano took me to the hotel early the next morning, the canals were empty. The pink light of morning seemed to be kissing the city awake.

Stefano helped me onto the dock by the hotel and tenderly kissed me goodbye. I couldn't speak. I could barely swallow for the lump in my throat. I waved as Stefano turned the boat around and sped away.

I spent my last night in Venice alone at the hotel. The maids had left a collection of chocolates on the bed table, one for each night I hadn't slept there. My breakfast tray arrived at the usual time the next morning. There were two red roses in the vase, with a note from Enrico saying *we are sorry this is your last day with us.*

He was at the front desk when I went to check out.

"I have a message for you," he said, pulling an envelope from a drawer beneath the counter.

The paper had the sumptuous texture of linen. The message baffled me at first. It was from Stefano.

Enrico watched me as I read. When I finished, he said, "He loved that you didn't know."

"I feel so foolish."

"Don't feel foolish, *signora*. His life is full of people who adore him for the wrong reasons."

My tenor was famous in Venice. He had made his debut two

years earlier at La Fenice, Stefano told me, and suddenly his career had exploded.

"He said was going to Milan yesterday on business for his father," I said.

"Maybe that was a little lie." Enrico smiled. "He's performing at La Scala this fall. I think rehearsals begin soon."

"But singing on the gondola..."

"He used to sing on his cousin's gondola in his student days. He doesn't do it often anymore. But when he does, he donates the tips he gets to charities. Venetians love him."

I shook my head. "I was so stupid."

Enrico squeezed my hand. "No, no. You had a beautiful affair. There's nothing stupid about that."

~5~

Abundance

I hadn't heard from Gavin in a long while, not since I had filed for divorce. After I returned from Venice, he called me to say he was coming to L.A. on business. He must have been shocked when I said yes to his lunch invitation.

He wanted to meet at the Ritz Carlton in Pasadena, which I thought was a bit over the top. Canapés and harp music were quite an upgrade for us. I would have preferred a back booth in a dark bar where I didn't feel on display.

I had a bad case of butterflies as I stepped out of the car and handed the keys to the valet attendant. I smoothed the wrinkles from my linen skirt. It was a hot day. My skirt and I were both looking a bit wilted.

Gavin and I hadn't seen each other in nine years. But the second I saw him, reading a newspaper on a sofa in the lobby, it seemed like time had stood still. He looked the same, except for streaks of gray in his still thick, wavy hair. He had the glow of a tan and when he stood up, I could see he was still fit. He looked fabulous, in fact. The butterflies flapped their wings harder.

I felt strangely stuck to the marble floor, afraid I might slip if I took a step. In a few long strides, Gavin had me in his arms. For the first time since my divorce, I thought I might cry, really cry.

Seconds after we sat down at a table on the patio, he saw I wasn't wearing my wedding ring.

"Laura," he said, clearing his throat. "Should I pretend I haven't noticed?" He reached over and took my ringless hand in his.

I told him an abbreviated version of what happened. He held onto my hand as I spoke and when I finished, he said, "Would you like a Scotch?"

"I'd love one."

We were back, Gavin and I. I don't remember what we had for lunch or what songs the harpist played. Gavin ordered champagne after dessert and asked the waiter to have the bottle sent to his room, where we made love the rest of the afternoon.

As he brought me to a climax that day, I felt swept away by the memories of us in New York. I remembered the pain of our last time together, unable to imagine then that we'd ever get another chance at love.

But there we were at the Ritz on a day in late summer, in a tangle of bedsheets. Anything seemed possible. Or so I thought.

When I started seeing Gavin again, Kyle was five.

Ryan had moved out of the house at the start of the separation and lived close by, which had its drawbacks. He was inclined to unplanned visits and would get angry with me when I'd remind him that we had a visitation schedule.

Kyle didn't seem to miss Ryan. Ever since that horrible day at the beach, he had withdrawn from Ryan, who tried – almost too hard – to please him. But Kyle was wary.

As the separation continued, Kyle was prone to meltdowns. What provoked them seemed innocuous, but I soon learned Kyle was wired a lot like me. The tears often had nothing to do with the situation at hand.

Gavin and I had discussed how to handle our relationship in my shaky post-divorce life. Gavin wanted us to be out in the open, but I wasn't ready for that. He was coming to L.A. routinely – twice a month – and staying at the Ritz. One Saturday afternoon, Gavin and I bumped into several of my girlfriends who had gathered in the Ritz's tearoom for a baby shower – an invitation I had declined. I could see by the expressions on their faces that my secret wasn't mine to keep any longer.

I knew I needed to tell Ryan before he heard the gossip. When he brought Kyle back to the house later that afternoon, I broke the news. At first, he was speechless, but then a barrage of questions gave way to a tirade.

Gavin was in my study at the back of the house when the outburst began. He came running to the front porch where Ryan and I were arguing. When Ryan saw Gavin standing in the doorway of the house that once had been his, he burst into tears and cried, "You son of a bitch!"

Our lives were awash in tears.

In the months that followed, Gavin and I tried to get our footing as a couple, but it was difficult.

I was so intent on being a good mother that I couldn't – or wouldn't – put Gavin's needs first. He was never demanding. But understandably, his patience wore thin when I had trouble making time for him.

Christmas that year brought everything to a head. Insanely, my mother had invited Ryan to come with Kyle and me for Christmas.

I was furious when Ryan told me she had called to tell him my father would pay for our airline tickets, which seemed more manipulative than generous to me.

"Why is this a problem?" she asked me in a heated phone conversation.

"Mom, have you forgotten that Ryan and I are divorced?"

"You don't have to sleep together. We have plenty of room."

"Kyle and I won't be coming for Christmas. Hope you have a nice time with Ryan. Goodbye, Mom."

I was shaking when I slammed down the phone. It rang a few seconds later, but I didn't answer.

Ryan called me later that day to assure me he wouldn't be going to Chicago for Christmas. "Can we try to have our own Christmas here?"

"How would that work?"

"I could come over on Christmas morning to open presents. Would you be okay with that?"

"Yes, I'd be okay with that."

A few days later, Gavin booked a room at the Ritz for Christmas week. I suddenly felt overwhelmed, trying to manage everyone's holiday expectations.

My family was broken. My heart was broken. I had no idea how to create a merry Christmas.

Somehow, we got through the day. Kyle was delighted with his presents from Santa and Ryan seemed happy having Christmas morning *en famille*. The definition of family had changed for us all. My parents clearly suffered with that new definition. Our phone conversation that day was frostier than the weather in Chicago.

Gavin came over later that afternoon. We made a big pizza – I hadn't lost my dough-making skill. Kyle decorated it with a Christmas tree made of slices of green pepper and pepperoni. I loved that Christmas dinner, with Gavin and Kyle. It gave me hope that new traditions would come and that maybe one day my heart would feel whole again.

I was a single mom, on active duty, for 13 years. Ryan traveled a lot in his work and tried his best to be an involved dad when he was in town. But mostly I was the parent-in-charge.

At first, I felt conspicuous in my community of school moms as a divorced woman. I sensed that I was envied by some who were unhappy in their marriages. But for years, I was the odd duck. I grew used to that and didn't mind sitting out the dances at the gala fund-raisers, though after a few of those events, I stopped going all together.

My rekindled romance with Gavin lasted for a year. Ironically, it was during my first time with him in London that we broke up. We had planned the visit for months. I had stopped over in Chicago to deliver Kyle to my parents for a two-week stay and had boarded my connecting flight feeling like I might explode from giddiness. My first few days with Gavin were like a honeymoon. I suppose it was the perfectness of it that unraveled us. We saw what could be, but knew it wasn't something we could sustain.

It was Gavin who ended it. He did it gently, swearing he'd love me forever. I stoically agreed it was for the best, but I cried all the way back to Chicago.

Life went on. I dated some, but nothing lasted. I threw myself into my writing and got a novel published. I found solace in the worlds I invented on my laptop screen, vicariously living through the fascinating lives of my characters.

When Kyle was a teenager and going off on his own adventures in the summers, I started traveling to Europe for two to three weeks at a time. It was my dream to live abroad for a couple of years after Kyle went to college, so I regarded these vacations as location-scouting trips. I traveled to France and Spain, but it was Italy that reeled me in once again.

The weekend of Kyle's high-school graduation, I took my parents, who had come for the occasion, out for lunch.

"I have an announcement to make," I said after our cocktails were served. "When Kyle leaves for college in the fall, I'm going to Italy."

My mom smiled. "That's nice, honey. How long will you be gone?"

"Maybe a year, if I can get a visa for an extended stay."

"A year? What about Kyle?"

"Mom, he'll be at school."

"But you'll be so far away."

"We'll be able to talk on skype. If there's an emergency, I can be home in a day."

"What about Christmas?"

"We can all meet up for Christmas, Mom."

She seemed relieved. "Ryan, too?"

I wanted to shake her. "Mom, stop."

But there was no stopping her. "I still don't understand why you divorced him, Laura."

After 13 years, she was still angry with me for destroying her sense of family.

After Kyle left for college, I settled in Florence with a couple of suitcases and a few boxes of books. I had sold the house and put what few belongings I had kept in storage. I felt light and free, ready to embrace a new chapter of my life.

My sister, Emily, came to visit me several months after I arrived in Florence. She was recovering from a break-up with her partner, a French woman named Renée. I hadn't spent much time with Emily in a couple of years, though we occasionally spoke on skype. My parents had pretty much disowned her when she came out in her early 30s. Actually, it was my mother who had turned away from her and my father did the same to keep peace with my mother.

Emily was bright and funny, always up for a good time. But I quickly realized during her first couple of days in Florence that the spark had gone out of my sister.

One night over a dinner of spaghetti and Chianti she told me she had recently been diagnosed with Stage 3 breast cancer. Her chemo treatments would begin when she got back to the States.

"This is my last fling," she said bravely.

She looked so lovely in the candlelight that I wouldn't let myself believe that cancer was eating away at her.

I reached for her hand. "How long have you known?"

"A few weeks."

"I assume you haven't told Mom and Dad."

She shook her head. "No. And you'll not tell them either. I need you to promise me that."

"But Emily..."

"Laura, I need your word."

"Okay. I won't tell them."

Emily lived in Baltimore and would be getting her treatments at Johns Hopkins. Medically, I knew she'd be in good hands, but she needed someone to be with her. Without Renée in her life, I knew that person should be me.

At first, Emily objected to the idea of having me come. But I insisted. I'd lost a close friend to breast cancer a few years earlier and knew how sick Emily would be.

"Let me come for the first month and we'll see how you do," I said.

She finally agreed. I flew back to Baltimore with her and stayed for three months.

She had a violent reaction to the chemotherapy. One day after a treatment, I found her clinging to the toilet bowl in her bathroom, sobbing.

"I can't do this, Laura."

I wiped the tears and vomit from her face. "It will get better. You'll get better. It's just horrible right now."

"I have nothing to live for." Those words came out of her like the bleating cry of a wounded animal.

Emily had lost the love of her life. In my eyes, Renée was a coward who had abandoned Emily in her darkest hour. For Emily, the light in her soul had been snuffed out the day she told Renée about her diagnosis.

Emily's cancer progressed quickly because she couldn't tolerate the treatments. After one scan, her oncologist met with me privately. "The only thing we can do at this point is make her comfortable," he said. "I'd recommend starting hospice care."

For me, the agonizing part of Emily's last weeks, aside from losing my only sibling, was honoring my promise not to tell our parents. During those three months, I hadn't even told them I was in Baltimore. I managed to fool them into thinking I was skyping with them from Italy. Sometimes, I could hear Emily chuckling in the next room when I'd give them the weather report from Florence.

Kyle came to visit Emily on his spring break, a week before she died. They'd had a wonderful relationship when he was growing up. She was the doting aunt and he, the boy who adored her spunk and sparkle. On their last visit together, he was the doting nephew who told her ribald stories about his college life that made her laugh.

On the night before he left, he held her hand and mine. "I'll be a lucky man if I ever find a woman as wonderful as you both are."

"We're the lucky ones," Emily said.

More than once, I was tempted to call my parents during Emily's final days. But I knew if they arrived at the end, it would deny her the peace she wanted.

Emily was on a morphine drip the day before she died when Renée called out of the blue.

"Emily?" she asked, sounding puzzled by my voice.

"No, this is her sister."

"It's Renée. Is she there?"

Not for much longer, you bitch, I was tempted to say. "Yes, but she can't talk right now."

"Would you tell her I called? I'll be home this evening."

"I'll tell her."

I went to Emily's bedside and stroked her hand. "That was Renée on the phone."

Emily was asleep, but her eyelids fluttered at the mention of Renée's name.

"She said to tell you she's been thinking about you and would like you to call her back when you can."

I embellished just a little, but just enough to make Emily smile through her morphine-induced haze.

And the next day, Emily was gone.

Predictably, I had holy hell to pay with my mother. My father was too heartbroken to lash out at me. I compressed the timeline of Emily's illness to make it sound more sudden. They arrived the next day and my mother took charge of the funeral arrangements, as I knew she would. Emily had asked that I read her favorite poem, *Sleeping in the Forest* by Mary Oliver, at the service. My mother wept as I recited the poem from memory, standing beside my sister's casket:

> *I thought the earth*
> *remembered me, she*
> *took me back so tenderly, arranging*
> *her dark skirts, her pockets*
> *full of lichens and seeds. I slept*
> *as never before, a stone*
> *on the riverbed, nothing*
> *between me and the white fire of the stars*
> *but my thoughts, and they floated*
> *light as moths among the branches*
> *of the perfect trees. All night*
> *I heard the small kingdoms breathing*
> *around me, the insects, and the birds*
> *who do their work in the darkness. All night*
> *I rose and fell, as if in water, grappling*
> *with a luminous doom. By morning*
> *I had vanished at least a dozen times*
> *into something better.*

Renée, who sat at the back of the church, wept, too.

I returned to Florence, feeling gutted by loss.

I wrote reams in the weeks after Emily's death, trying to make sense of what had happened to her. I wondered if her broken heart had triggered her cancer, and I hated Renée even more for the possibility of that.

Renée had become Emily's reason for being. As beautiful as love can be, at what point is it capable of becoming toxic? When had Emily lost herself in her love for this woman she idolized?

I thought a lot about love in those lonely days of my grieving. I realized I had nearly given up hope of finding the kind of love I longed for – something true and lasting, built to weather flooding lagoons and hailstorms.

To console myself, I booked a trip to Venice. It was a sunny June day when I walked out of the Santa Lucia train station on the Grand Canal, exactly 14 years since my last visit.

I didn't stay at the same *pensione*. I wanted to explore another part of Venice. This wasn't meant to be a journey of retracing my own footsteps.

But I found myself outside La Fenice on my second day. *Turandot* was on and Venice's favorite tenor was appearing as Calaf. I bought a ticket for that evening's performance.

Stefano was amazing. As he sang "Nessun Dorma," I closed my eyes and remembered another day when he serenaded a wet-haired maiden in her terrycloth bathrobe.

After the performance, I stood with a large group of fans at the back of the opera house where an ornate gondola was moored at the dock. A cheer went up when Stefano appeared with his leading lady, the despicable Princess Turandot. Actually, without her stage makeup, she looked sweet and lovely. Stefano held her hand as the gondolier helped her onto the boat, and then he turned to the crowd and waved. I thought for a second, when he looked in my direction, there was a flicker of something. But I think it was just my heart skipping a beat.

Emily's death broke something inside my mother. I'm sure of that, looking back now.

My father told me the changes were subtle at first. He thought it was just the memory loss that comes with age. My mother called them her "senior moments" and laughed when she'd forget the day of the week or how old she was.

The summer after Emily died, Kyle and I went to see my parents. When Kyle walked in the door, my mother asked, "Who are you?"

Kyle thought she was joking and said, "Grammy, it's me. Kyle. Your grandson."

She looked befuddled. "My grandson is a little boy." She turned to a bulletin board above her desk in the kitchen and unpinned a photo of Kyle from grade school. "This is my grandson."

It was like watching combustible fabric go up in flames. In her lucid moments, she seemed herself, but then she'd tell you a fantastical story about being held hostage at the grocery store. One night, she ran through the house screaming that there was a strange man in her bed. Of course, that man was my father.

My dad and I spoke with the family doctor who recommended a psychiatric evaluation. But Mom wasn't far gone enough not to know that her mental faculties were under scrutiny.

"You think I'm going crazy, don't you?" she yelled at me after her first session with the psychiatrist.

I found her one afternoon sitting on the porch cradling a baby doll that had belonged to Emily and me.

"Shhh," my mom whispered as I sat down beside her. "I just got your sister to sleep." She kissed the doll's forehead. "My precious little Emily."

I stayed with my parents that summer, trying to help them through their living nightmare. But there was no escape from it. Mom needed full-time care. My father couldn't bear for her to be admitted to a psychiatric hospital. But as her dementia worsened, she became increasingly frightened and violent. By the end of the summer, her psychiatrist persuaded my dad to sign the papers.

It was a lovely facility with a caring staff. They found a mix of meds that quieted Mom. She was calmer. Her scary fantasies went away. But she held on to the baby doll she called Emily.

My dad visited her every day. His devotion to my mother as her mind faded away was the greatest testament to love I've ever known.

Both my sister and father died of broken hearts. It was cancer that killed Emily in the end. It was a stroke that took my father a few days before Christmas the same year that Emily died. He had been sitting in the living room listening to a CD of Christmas music I had given him. He went peacefully, in my mom's favorite red-leather chair.

My mother hung on for almost a year. I imagined her world as a foggy forest, where bright sunlight sometimes burned through the mist. Once in a while, she seemed to recognize me. But then she'd say, "I don't know anyone named Laura."

As I cleared out my parents' house, I found a box of their college mementos – photos, a yearbook, a bundle of letters and my mother's dance cards from her sorority parties. My father, in his immaculate handwriting, had claimed every dance. He wasn't going to give another guy a chance.

I lingered over their wedding album one rainy afternoon. I turned to the last page, to dad's heroic save on the steps as they headed off on their honeymoon. He loved her and protected her till his dying day. A gallant man true to his word.

I returned to Florence after Mom died and tried not to dwell on loss and regret. I settled into my life there, grateful that I had a new place to call home. I made friends. I traveled a lot. But I spent a lot of time alone. One day that changed.

It was a chilly spring afternoon and I was missing those beautiful gloves that I had left in a taxi driven by a card shark named Niccolò.

I stopped in at Madova. The sales clerk smiled as I placed my hand on the golden cushion. "Seven and a half," she said. I chose a pair of cashmere-lined gloves the color of pomegranates.

As I left the shop, I turned up my coat collar, with my new gloves on. There was an invigorating nip in the air.

I noticed an older couple, in their 70s, walking ahead of me, arm-in-arm. The man brushed his cheek against hers and stole a kiss.

In a painfully truthful moment, I would admit that the biggest regret of my life is not falling in love in my youth with a man I'd grow to love even more as we aged together. I've often wondered about all the times I've said no to possibilities, turning away from chance, from a love that might have been. Sometimes I feel I've spent a lifetime looking in vain for true and lasting love.

But in that moment, I had a realization. Truth be told, I had experienced love in abundance.

I realized how much richer my life had been for the happiness love had shown me, even if it wasn't lasting. I had experienced intimacy and tenderness that had given me a gentle heart, and even in the despair of lost love, I hadn't lost hope that true love would find me.

When I reached the piazza in my neighborhood, I saw a man, obscured by a newspaper, sitting at a café table. I glanced at my watch. He was early.

In my handbag, I had a letter that had arrived in my mailbox a week earlier. I had recognized the handwriting immediately and wondered, in astonishment, how he had he found me after all these years. Indeed love works in mysterious ways.

As I walked across the piazza, the man looked up from his paper and grinned. His hair had turned gray and the lines in his face were deeper. But his alluring smile was the same.

He stood and embraced me. "If I were Marcello Mastroianni, I'd take you back to my villa and make love to you," he said.

I kissed Gavin's cheek. "Sounds divine, *amore*."

37045254R00093

Made in the USA
Columbia, SC
03 December 2018